# A BOOK ABOUT
# BUPKES*

*nothing

**To Joni—a good editor is not *bubkes*. —L.K.**
**For Mom and Dad, from Rx —R.d.R.**

KAR-BEN PUBLISHING®
An imprint of Lerner Publishing Group, Inc.
241 First Avenue North
Minneapolis, MN 55401 USA

Website address: www.karben.com

Main body text set in Imperfect OT.
Typeface provided by T26.

**Library of Congress Cataloging-in-Publication Data**

Names: Kimmelman, Leslie, author. | De Rond, Roxana, illustrator.
Title: A book about bupkes / Leslie Kimmelman ; illustrated by Roxana De Rond.
Description: Minneapolis, MN : Kar-Ben Publishing, [2023] | "Bupkes: nothing at all. The word is Yiddish, a language that was once spoken by the Jews of Eastern Europe and elsewhere around the world. Some people still speak Yiddish today." | Audience: Ages 4–8. | Audience: Grades K–1. | Summary: "This is a book about bupkes: nothing, zero, zilch. An empty garden, an empty bench at the playground, an empty soup bowl all seem like nothing - bupkes! The funny thing is that bupkes may mean nothing - but it can feel like everything"— Provided by publisher.
Identifiers: LCCN 2022041786 (print) | LCCN 2022041787 (ebook) | ISBN 9781728460222 (library binding) | ISBN 9781728460291 (paperback) | ISBN 9781728495583 (ebook)
Subjects: LCSH: Bupkes (The English word)—Juvenile literature. | English language—Foreign elements—Yiddish—Juvenile literature.
Classification: LCC PE1599.B87 K56 2023 (print) | LCC PE1599.B87 (ebook) | DDC 428.1—dc23/eng/20230111

LC record available at https://lccn.loc.gov/2022041786
LC ebook record available at https://lccn.loc.gov/2022041787

Manufactured in the United States of America
1-51484-50369-11/21/2022

# A BOOK ABOUT
# BUPKES*

*nothing

The word "bupkes" is Yiddish, a language that was once spoken by the Jews of Eastern Europe and elsewhere around the world. Some people still speak Yiddish today.

Leslie Kimmelman

illustrated by Roxana de Rond

KAR-BEN
PUBLISHING

This book is about **bupkes.**

That's right.

**Bupkes.**

Nothing!

Zero.

Zilch.

# Bupkes!

The thing about bupkes, though, is that it can be tricky. Sometimes something that looks like bupkes—nothing—is actually something.

Look at all the vegetables growing! Zoe and her mom fill their baskets with delicious food. Until . . .

**Bupkes!**

The garden is empty, but . . .

their neighbor is happy.

What a mess! There is so much trash in the park.

Until Zoe and her friends arrive, and soon . . .

**Bupkes!**

No trash.

But what a beautiful park.

Zoe's kitchen is kind of a mess too.

But little by little,

dish by dish,

splash by splish,

swash by swish,

pop by pop . . .

**Bupkes!**
No dirty dishes.
But a sparkling clean kitchen!

There's no room for anything—
or anyone—else.

Until Zoe introduces herself, and then . . .

**Bupkes!**
Empty bench. Full hearts.

Zoe has filled a big bowl to the brim with hot,
delicious, sneezing-and-sniffling-curing chicken soup.

Until, before long . . .

*Slurp, slurp, slurp*—**bupkes!**

Mommy feels so much better.

The thing is, **bupkes** may mean nothing . . .

. . . but it can feel like everything!

WOLFGANG AMADEUS MOZART 1756 1956

# MOZART

## *and*

## *Prague*

Buchner, Alexandr

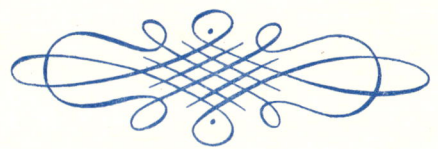

ARTIA

MOZART AND PRAGUE

by

Alexander Buchner, Karel Koval, Karel Mikysa, Antonín Čubr

Translated by Daphne Rusbridge

Jacket and binding by Vojtěch Kubašta

Designed and produced by ARTIA, Prague

(A - 45)

Printed in Czechoslovakia

In 1956 the 200th anniversary of the birth of Wolfgang Amadeus Mozart was celebrated throughout the world. "There is no other name among the great musicians which is pronounced with such universal, unanimous and sincere respect and love as that of Mozart," wrote Otakar Hostinský, the Czech musicologist, in 1887, on the occasion of the 100th anniversary of the world première of *Don Giovanni* in Prague. Particularly in the hearts of the Czech people Mozart's name strikes a chord, and history records but few cases of an artist receiving such understanding and love outside his own country as Mozart received in Prague. That his music was a success was no accident: it was not due to the whim and fancy of the Prague audience; the reason lies deep down in the roots of Czech music culture. Prague welcomed Mozart with open arms and it had a right to the proud title of The City of Mozart. The German historian Arthur Schurig, who was Mozart's biographer, admits that the Prague audience played an important part in Mozart's life and in his works subsequent to *Figaro*. He writes: "It was in fact in the capital of Bohemia that Mozart was for the first time fully understood, valued and loved. If any town has the right to be called his city, then it is not Salzburg which W. A. Mozart hated, it is not Vienna which left him to starve and forgot him in a mass grave, but only his golden Prague."

## BOHEMIA, THE CONSERVATOIRE OF EUROPE

The most valuable testimony to the musicianship of the Czech nation is to be found in Charles Burney's notes on "The Present State of Music in Germany". On his travels through Europe, the British musician and writer also visited Bohemia, which had long attracted him. He wrote that he had often heard that the Czechs were the most musically talented nation in Germany, indeed perhaps in all of Europe. A famous German composer (Johann Christian Bach), who was at that time in London, had assured him that if the Czechs had as favourable conditions as the Italians, they would surely outclass them.

Burney travelled the length and breadth of the Kingdom of Bohemia and observed with great interest how music was taught to the ordinary people. In Čáslav at the house of the famous organist and teacher, Jan Dusík, he noticed in one of the rooms a number of girls and boys from 6 to 11 years of age reading, writing and making music on the violin, the oboe, the double bass and other instruments. There were four pianos in this room and a boy was seated at each of them. As far back as the 18th century,

Burney drew the attention of the world to this school, modestly hidden away, to the secret roots of Czech musicianship which penetrated all the villages, the small and larger towns where Czech music teachers nurtured the musical traditions of which they were the guardians.

Many Czech musicians left their country, where servility, social oppression and counter-reformation persecution irked them, for Germany, Italy, Russia or France. Thus Bohemia became known as the *conservatoire* of Europe. One of the most famous of these musical emigrants was Jan Václav Stamic (1717 to 1757) of Německý Brod. Stamic's father, who was also his teacher, gave him a thorough grounding in music and made him a splendid musician; he was the founder of the Mannheim school, which was famous throughout Europe, and acted as a magnet on all contemporary composers who were searching for new paths in music. J. Ch. Bach and above all Mozart were of their number. Mannheim was a turning point for him and it remained an inspiration throughout his further life.

## VILLAGE TEACHERS AND ORGANISTS: THE CREATORS OF THE CZECH TRADITION

The village teachers were the cultivators of the musical youth of Bohemia. In Prague the choirmasters and organists took the pick of the country singers and sensitive violinists for the monasteries and the church choirs where instrumental music was cultivated with such love and diligence that all who heard it were amazed at the masterly achievements of the ordinary Czechs. The successor of Bohuslav Černohorský, the Czech composer known in Italy as the *Padre Boemo* (1684–1742), was Josef Seger (1716 to 1782), an organist known throughout Europe. Josef Mysliveček, Jan Křtitel Kuchař, abbé Josef Jelínek and Jan Antonín Koželuh (who later became friends of Mozart) were among his pupils. Another outstanding organist and composer was František Václav Habermann (1706–1783), whose mass was played in England, where G. F. Handel himself copied it. Handel liked the themes so much that he made use of a number of them in his oratorio, *Jephthah*. Habermann was the first teacher of Josef Mysliveček and František Xaver Dušek. Nor should the modest but great organist and composer, and conductor of the choir of St. Vitus's Cathedral in Prague, František Xaver Brixi (1732–1771), be forgotten. His father, Šimon Brixi, the choirmaster, (1693–1735) was the brother of Dorothy Benda, mother of the famous Benda.

Mozart esteemed the works of F. X. Brixi very highly. During his stay in Prague he asked J. A. Koželuh, the choirmaster at St. Vitus's cathedral, to show him the music archives. It was cold down there and for that reason he kept his hat on. Of all the music contained in the archives, the Graduale – a G-minor fugue by F. X. Brixi written for the Fourth Sunday after Easter – struck Mozart most. He was perusing Brixi's Graduale, when he suddenly took his three-cornered hat, made a sweeping bow and cried out: "You have to take off your hat to a man like Brixi!"

## CZECH FRIENDS IN MOZART'S LIFE

Let us now take a look at Mozart's direct links with Bohemia. From his childhood to his last days, the names of Czech musicians appear in Mozart's life like the blooms of a hundred-petalled rose. As a small boy, staring with a boy's inquisitiveness at the musicians in the archiepiscopal orchestra, Mozart recognised two outstanding Czech musicians, Dražil and Sádlo, who were frequent guests of the Mozart family and who visited Amadeus and his father in Vienna even at a time when there was a serious danger of small pox, as a letter from Olomouc, written by Mozart's father, Leopold, and dated November 1769, testifies. Dražil, a horn player, and Sádlo, a bassoon player, had been schooled in the Czech wind instruments tradition, which was famous throughout Europe and the pride of the Mannheim school, and had been introduced into Paris by J. V. Stamic. At Christmas time, Czech musicians used to play folk *pastorales* at Salzburg; the motif of one must have remained in Mozart's memory, since he used it in his ballet, *Les petits riens*, written in Paris in 1777:

In Vienna, at the court of Maria Theresa, the seven-year-old Mozart got to know the court composer Georg Christopher Wagenseil, and his pupil and successor Josef Antonín Štěpán (1726–1800), who was an outstanding pianist and composer and the teacher of Maria Theresa's children. Here too he met František Tůma, composer to the Emperor's widow, Elisabeth Christina. Štěpán set Goethe's poem, *The Violet*, to music in 1774; he loved the same things as Mozart.

Of the greatest importance in the life of the fourteen-year-old Mozart was his meeting with Josef Mysliveček in Bologna. Mysliveček, then thirty years of age, was known through Italy as *Il divino Boemo*. In a letter written by Leopold Mozart from Bologna on the 4th August, 1770, we read: "Mr. Mysliveček has been here. Mysliveček has been commissioned by Milan for the first carnival opera of 1772, i. e., one year after Wolfgang." What the talks and conversations between the Mozarts and the Myslivečeks meant to the friends is clear from a letter dated 27th October, 1770, in which Leopold, Mozart's father, wrote to his wife and his daughter, Anna, in Salzburg: "Mr. Mysliveček frequently comes to see us in Bologna and we go to see him. He is writing an oratorio for Padua which will soon be finished; after that he will leave for Bohemia. He is an honourable man and we have struck up a warm friendship." That it was not merely a superficial friendship, we see from the extraordinarily extensive correspondence which is proof of close co-operation between Mozart and Mysliveček. Unfortunately some of the letters have been lost, but even so there are 32 letters which provide the most detailed information about Mozart's relations with the musicians in his life. How great Mozart's interest was in the symphonic works of Mysliveček is clear from a postscript added by Wolfgang Amadeus to a letter from his father to his mother, dated December 22nd, 1770: "Ask whether they have got this symphony of Mysliveček's in Salzburg. If not, we shall bring it with us." And he added in his characteristic manuscript the following four introductory bars of Mysli-veček's symphony for his mother:

## THE DUŠEKS

The most fateful encounter between Mozart and any Czech musician was his meeting with the Dušeks. Mrs. Josefa Dušek, the daughter of a Prague apothecary, Hambacher, was an excellent singer, and her husband, F. X. Dušek, was a piano virtuoso, composer and a splendid teacher who had to his credit a number of outstanding pupils (Leopold Koželuh, Jan Nepomuk Vitásek, Vincenc Mašek, etc.). In the *Jahrbuch der Tonkunst von Wien und Prag* of 1796 we read: "František Dušek, that great virtuoso and composer for piano, fully deserves the title Professor of Music, for in him Prague has not only a man who has trained a large number of master musicians, but one who can rightly be called a pillar of the art of music which has hitherto held its own." Dušek is considered to be the founder of the oldest Czech piano school; his playing was characterised by a light touch, by a gentle and expressive performance. As a com-poser he worked in every field of music (over 300 of his works have been preserved). It is also decidedly worthy of note that his works, most of which were written during the sixties of the 18th century, bear the same melodic character as Mozart's. Thus next to Johann Christian Bach and J. Mysliveček, Dušek can be said to be Mozart's closest predecessor.

The Dušeks played a most important part in the life of Mozart, both in the creative and the human sense of the word. From the day that they met in the summer of 1777 to the end of his life in 1791, he shared all his experiences with them, as though he had been a member of the family and after his death it was they who cared for the homeless orphans he left behind. It was the Dušeks who recognised behind Mozart's first great fight, prior to the première of *The Marriage of Figaro* in Vienna in April 1786, the treachery of the Italian clique, the 'cabal' which with honeyed smile made his work impossible and was so jealous of his successes that *Figaro* soon disappeared from the repertoire. Mozart was on the point of leaving Vienna for England, when he suddenly decided to go to Prague. And we must state here that this was thanks to the Dušeks who insisted on *Figaro* being staged at the Nostitz Theatre, where the opera was outstandingly successful.

## MANNHEIM CZECHS AND VIENNESE CZECHS

From Mannheim Mozart wrote to his father about the impression which Jiří Benda's melodramas had made on him. At the first hearing, they moved him like nothing else, during his travels through Germany, Italy, France, England, Holland and Belgium. Seldom did Mozart use such extravagant words as he used in speaking of Benda's melodramas *Medea* and *Ariadne on Naxos*. It is clear from his notes that here he came into contact with something about which he had dreamed but which he did not think could be realised. Jiří Benda, musician and thinker, director of the Duke's music in Gotha, Thuringia, by origin a Czech, in a flash provided a convincing answer to his burning question. Mozart became so fond of Benda that he spoke of him as his darling and took his works along with him on his travels. On 3rd December, 1778, a few days after his first feeling of delight at Benda's melodramas, he wrote from Mannheim to Salzburg: "Oh, if we only had clarinets! You wouldn't believe how incredibly beautiful such a symphony is with flutes, oboes and clarinets." And he looked forward to introducing them into Salzburg immediately on his return. Rich indeed was the contribution of the Mannheim school and the pioneer work of Benda.

Here, we close the list of musicians and composers from Bohemia with whom Mozart came into contact on his travels through Europe. There is no space in this short introduction to deal with all of them, but at least the Viennese Czechs deserve to be mentioned: Václav Pichl (1741–1805), Archduke Ferdinand's own composer, about whom Nissen, who married Mozart's widow, wrote that most of Mozart's earlier instrumental works bear the stamp of Pichl's taste and manner of playing; František Adam Míča (1746–1811), of whose works Mozart performed a number at the court of Vienna. When a new symphony by Míča was anonymously performed in Vienna at President Keese's, Mozart, who was present, immediately declared that he knew the bird by his feathers, and in proof of his recognition he embraced Míča before the entire company. In Vienna Mozart made friends with the oboe and viola da gamba virtuoso, Josef Fiala (1748–1816). Vaňhal, abbé J. Jelínek and V. Jírovec are mentioned in the pictorial part of this publication. There remain to be mentioned the brothers Vranický: Pavel (1756–1825) (note the connection between his *Oberon* and Mozart's *Magic Flute*!) and Antonín (1761–1820); F. X. Vošitka; Antonín Rössler-Rosetti (1750–1792); J. Rejcha (1745–1795); J. Janič, and F. Hejna. But those whose names are not mentioned here—and there are many of them—were on the best terms with Mozart and with one exception were his friends. That exception was Leopold Koželuh who joined forces with Salieri and went over to the camp of Mozart's enemies. But this single shadow fades away in the light of the sincere love of the Czechs for Mozart which finally brought him to their capital, a capital which had no king but which was itself called *Praga regina musicae*. And Prague, the Queen of Music, received Mozart with love and understanding.

## MOZART TAKES PRAGUE BY STORM

Thanks are due to František Xaver Němeček, the first biographer of W. A. Mozart, for having recorded for all time that particular atmosphere in Prague in which Mozart felt at home, and where, in gratitude to a public which was the first to understand his music completely and without reservations, he wrote that opera of operas, *Don Giovanni*. Němeček faithfully recorded the enthusiastic reception given to *Il Seraglio*, Mozart's early opera, which was performed in Prague in 1783. "It seemed to us that what we had heard and known hitherto was not music at all. Everyone was carried away, everyone was in transports at the new harmonies, at the original movements for wind instruments, the like of which had never been heard before" (cf. Mozart's enthusiasm about the clarinets, flutes and oboes in Mannheim).

"The Czechs began to hunt for his works and that very same year Mozart's piano compositions and symphonies were performed at all the better music academies. It was then that the Czechs acquired a taste for his works. The greatest musical experts of our town were at the same time the greatest admirers of Mozart, the most ardent heralds of his fame."

And when *The Marriage of Figaro* was performed in Prague (première 10th December, 1786), the enthusiasm waxed still stronger and all Prague was so enraptured by Mozart that his tunes could be heard from morning to night in the alehouse and on the street, in homes and in palaces, and naturally the cry of "Encore!" to the accompaniment of stormy applause never stopped in the Nostitz theatre. Even the harpist in the alehouse had to play *Non piu andrai* if he wished anyone to listen to him. The well-known Czech conductor of the opera orchestra, Josef Strobach (1731–1794), used to say that at each performance he and his orchestra came so under the spell of the music that notwithstanding the hard work they would have been delighted to start all over again. So great was the enthusiasm that Prague music lovers, headed by Jan Josef Count of Thun and the conductor Strobach, and his orchestra, decided to invite Mozart to Prague. They wrote a letter to him in Vienna together with a poem in his honour asking him to come and listen to a performance of his *Figaro*.

At that time Mozart had suffered a severe disappointment in Vienna. As a result of the intrigues of the Italian clique *Figaro* had been withdrawn to make way for other operas, whose composers had impressed the Emperor because of the laurels they had won in Italy and Paris. Mozart decided to travel again. The invitation from Prague fell like a ray of sun into his wintry musings at Christmas 1786. In December the papers published the news that Mozart was preparing to go to London "whence he has had a most advantageous offer, and he had decided to travel *via* Paris." But when he read the heart-warming news of the success of *Figaro* in Prague, Mozart decided to go to Bohemia, and immediately after the New Year he set out for the country of Mysliveček and Benda and of the "famous Czech wind instrumentalists"–the clarinet, oboe and bassoon players and the splendid players on the French horn (such as Jan Stich–Punto) whom he had met on his travels through Europe.

Mozart arrived in Prague on the 11th of January, 1787, with his wife, Constance, and his violinist brother-in-law, Fr. Hoffer. They went straight to the palace of their host, the Count of Thun, at midday. In the afternoon there was a concert in Mozart's honour. There for the first time he made the acquaintance of the Thun orchestra. He liked it so much that he wrote on the 15th of January, 1787, to his friend Jacquin in Vienna. "After lunch the old Count, Thun, honoured us with music made by his own people which lasted nearly an hour and half. I shall be able to enjoy this real pleasure every day." Mozart's comment on Prague musicians is the most eloquent testimony to the high level of the chamber orchestras of the day which vied with each other for the first place. A few hours later Mozart left for the Bretfeld Ball with M. Canal of Malabail and was astounded to see everybody dancing to his *Figaro*. The Czech aristocracy, Prague musicians, singers and audience, irrespective of estate and profession, all wanted to make his acquaintance, they all said so many nice things to him that his head swam when he compared this with the cold atmosphere of Vienna where shoulders were shrugged when his name was mentioned. Naturally Mozart's popularity was exploited to the full by the old Prague-Italian impresario, Pasquale Bondini. Within a few days he staged a performance of *Figaro* which, as Mozart was able to see for himself, had all the qualities of passion and musical precision he himself demanded.

The day after, Mozart himself conducted Strobach's splendid orchestra at the Nostitz theatre. He prepared to surprise the people of Prague with a symphony which he had brought from Vienna with the intention of performing it in Prague. On the 19th of January, 1787, a great musical celebration was held at the Nostitz theatre at which Mozart conducted the *Prague Symphony*. At the end he played the piano for at least half an hour improvising a fantasy which was welcomed with such a storm of applause as Prague had never known. Mozart had to go on playing. A fresh storm of applause broke out. Radiant with happiness he bowed to the audience. Suddenly from the stalls someone shouted: "Play something from *Figaro*." Whereupon Mozart conjured up before the breathless audience twelve variations on the aria *Non piu andrai* to thank his listeners for their sincere expression of heart-warming sympathy. F. X. Němeček wrote: "Surely just as this celebration was unique of its kind for the people of Prague, so for Mozart this day ranked among the most beautiful of his life." Mozart also expressed his satisfaction with the orchestra and he wrote them a letter which was read out by Němeček. Unfortunately, however, this has been lost. It was on that occasion that Mozart pronounced the memorable words: "My orchestra is in Prague. My Praguers understand me."

In the Prague merry-go-round Mozart could not find time to compose. Only Jan, count of Pachta, succeeded by cunning in getting him to write the dances he had promised him. He invited Mozart to lunch an hour ahead of time, and jokingly placed him under "house arrest", until such time as the dances should have been written. The manuscript is in Berlin and we read on the title page: *6 Tedeschi di W. A. Mozart, Prague 1787*. Shortly afterwards, however, Mozart wrote a theme of his own free will for the well-known Prague harpist, Haisler, as an expression of thanks for the variations on *Figaro* which this strolling musician played so splendidly in the "New Inn" in Prague Old Town unaware of the fact that the composer himself was listening to him. Mozart invited the harpist to his room and played him a new theme on the piano. This theme he dedicated to him. Haisler, whose nickname was "Pigtail", went from alehouse to alehouse with this theme until 1843, playing it as a message of love from "Mr. Mozart" to the people of Prague. This dedication shows how greatly Mozart valued the musicianship of the simple Czech musician.

Mozart remained in Prague till about the middle of February. Financially, too, he gained considerably. In a letter dated 12th January, 1787, his father, Leopold, wrote to Nannerl that her brother had received one thousand *gulden* for the musical celebration. Wherever he appeared he was greeted warmly and it was at that time that his decision was taken to thank the people of Prague by an opera dedicated to them. This spontaneous decision was most certainly supported not only by his musician-friends but also by the impresario, Quardasoni, for whom Mozart's opera dedicated to the people of Prague meant both the salvation of his coffers and a renewal of his contract with Count Nostitz for a further year.

During Mozart's very first visit to Prague, in addition to F. X. Dušek, three outstanding Prague musicians became his friends and faithful collaborators: the conductor of the opera orchestra, Josef Strobach, who conducted all Mozart's operas in Prague; Jan Křtitel Kuchař, a splendid organist and cembalo player, who was the first to arrange piano scores of *The Marriage of Figaro, Don Giovanni, Cosi fan Tutte, The Magic Flute* and *Titus* which were praised and enthusiastically received by Mozart, and lastly Václav Praupner, a noted composer—he wrote the melodrama *Circe*—organist and operatic choir-master who conducted all the choir parts of Mozart's operas in Prague. These three were completely devoted to Mozart. In them he found the strongest support and assistance for all his musical work in Prague.

# DON GIOVANNI – PREMIÈRE IN PRAGUE

Never had Mozart looked forward so greatly to the performance of a new opera as he did on leaving Vienna for Prague with the unfinished score of *Don Giovanni*.

Until recently it was not possible to establish the date of Mozart's second arrival in Prague precisely. Němeček states that he arrived in the winter, the lexicographer, J. B. Dlabač, notes that Mozart spent nearly the entire summer in Prague, while O. Jahn and H. Abert consider it probable that he left for Prague towards the end of August. Karel Koval believed that the 17th September was the correct date. Now, however, O. E. Deutsch has published two of Mozart's letters from the collection of M. G. Schnitzler, one of which was written to Mozart's brother-in-law, Berchtold Sonnenburg, about the estate of his father Leopold. It is headed Vienna, 29th September, 1787; it reads: "My dear brother. In great haste – I am most happy about our reconciliation. If you wish to send me a money order please address it to M. Michael Puchberg at Count Walsegg's house on the High Market, because the above-mentioned has a mandate to collect all monies for me, since I leave early Monday morning for Prague. May you be happy. A kiss from us both for our dear sister and rest assured that I shall always remain your loving brother, W. A. Mozart."

This letter proves that Mozart left Vienna for Prague on Monday, October 1st, 1787. Since the journey lasted about three days, Mozart's coach must have passed the Prague Gate on the 3rd October.

The première was fixed for 14th October to celebrate the presence of the Archduchess Maria Theresa, the bride of Prince Anton of Saxony; we can therefore well imagine how the rehearsals had to be rushed through to ensure that everything was ready and that everything went off smoothly and perfectly down to the last detail. The major part of the score had been written in Vienna. The overture, Masetto's aria No. 6, the Don Giovanni-Leporello duet No. 15 (the second act originally began with a recitative), and the entire second finale were written in Prague, as was Don Giovanni's serenade. The paper on which the parts of the opera composed in Prague were written is of a distinctly smaller size. The libretto was printed in Vienna, and from it we can see the great dramatic changes made in it by Mozart. It is shortened in places and added to in others to meet the requirements of the singers and of the production. Mozart himself attended the rehearsal of the entire opera. What importance Mozart attached to Prague's judgement is obvious from a conversation between Mozart and Kuchař, as they took a stroll together after the first rehearsal of *Don Giovanni*. Mozart asked Kuchař, who was to him not only a close friend but also an authority on music: "What do you think of the music of *Don Giovanni*? Will they like it as much as *Figaro*? It is quite different!" Kuchař answered: "How can you doubt it? The music is beautiful, original, and masterfully conceived. Anything of Mozart's cannot fail to delight the Czechs." Whereupon Mozart replied: "Your words reassure me; they come from an expert. Indeed I have spared no effort, no labour in order to be able to offer Prague something that is excellent."

The première of *Don Giovanni* was ill-fated. Three times it was put off because of a host of technical difficulties. Before it took place, Mozart conducted *The Marriage of Figaro* which was performed on Sunday, 14th October, instead of the première of *Don Giovanni* originally intended in honour of the

Archduchess Maria Theresa. Mozart spent a happy time with his musician friends who fulfilled his every wish. In between composing he played bowls at the Bertramka. In his boundless generosity he even found time to devote an hour each day to a talented singer, František Vladimír Hek, a student of philosophy who sang in the chorus in *Don Giovanni*; when Mozart discovered his talent for composition, he gave him lessons without taking any money for it, a none too frequent phenomenon in the history of music. This is indicative of Mozart's splendid attitude towards young Czech talent.

We shall not here repeat the well-known anecdotes describing how the overture was written in the night preceding the première, or how the concert aria, *Bella mia fiamma, addio!* came to be written, in which Mozart took leave of his dear friend, Mrs. Dušek, and of the city which had given him so much happiness and so much inspiration for his further work. The *première* held on the 29th of October, 1787, carried all before it. Not only did all the music lovers of Prague come to hear this opera of operas, but lovers of Mozart's music came from far and wide to attend the performance. For Mozart that evening was surely one of his happiest ones; *Don Giovanni* was acclaimed with unreserved warmth by the public. By dedicating *Don Giovanni* to the people of Prague, Mozart declared before the musical world his grateful love for the Prague audience which had understood him as no other audience before it, and his respect for the great Czech musical tradition with which his own work was bound up.

## MOZART'S THIRD AND FOURTH VISITS TO PRAGUE

The happy months in Prague were followed by lean times in Vienna. True, Mozart succeeded Gluck as court composer, but figures show clearly how his services were valued by the Emperor: Gluck received 2000 *gulden* yearly, Mozart only 800. The Viennese did not like *Don Giovanni*. They did not want Mozart's music at the Court, minuets for their balls excepted. Subscription lists also failed to bring in the desired number of subscribers. And so, in the gloomy year of 1788, Mozart wrote three beautiful symphonies–in E flat, in G minor, and in C–for his own consolation. Things looked black at home, and he gladly accepted the offer of his pupil, Prince Lichnovsky, to accompany him to northern Germany. Mozart hoped not only for financial advantages from this journey, but also the chance of a more permanent and lucrative employment than in Vienna. He arrived in Prague with Lichnovsky just past midday on Good Friday, April 10th, 1789, and although they spent only half a day there, he visited all the familiar places. Quardasoni immediately commissioned him to write an opera for the coming autumn and promised him 200 ducats in place of the usual 100, plus 50 travelling expenses. Mozart was delighted at the thought that he would again be writing for Prague. That same evening he wrote informing Constance before leaving for the north. At 9 o'clock in the evening he took leave of his friend, Dušek, and entered Lichnovsky's coach; it was on a mild April night that he passed through the Strahov gate along the road leading to Dresden. The concert tour lasted to the end of May. The financial results were very poor, and to crown everything Mozart was forced to lend Prince Lichnovsky 100 *gulden* out of his modest earnings, thereby paying for his seat in the coach as he would have done in any post-chaise. He returned to Prague on Sunday, 31st May. He could not sign the contract with Quardasoni because in the meantime the latter had left for Warsaw to take over the direction of the Italian opera. Thus his hopes of further work in Prague were dashed. This third and fourth visit to Prague were like friendly glimmerings of hope, which died down all too soon.

## THE CORONATION OPERA, THE MAGIC FLUTE, REQUIEM

Mozart's head was in a whirl when out of the blue the Czech Estates commissioned a Coronation opera *La Clemenza di Tito*. This was in the summer of 1791 when he was putting the finishing touches to *The Magic Flute* and he was greatly dismayed by the arrival of a mysterious messenger who came to commission the *Requiem*. What should he do first? Time was running short and his health was failing. But he couldn't deny Prague its request. Quardasoni had been to see Mozart about this opera in Vienna, in the middle of July, 1791, but a month had passed before the Marshall's Office confirmed the commission (evidently as a result of intrigues against Mozart) and Mozart received the definite decision just 18 days before the première was to be held in Prague.

Constance was only three weeks past childbirth, but she left the new-born Franz Xaver, and the 7 year old Karl Thomas with foster parents, and set out for Prague with Mozart and his pupil, Franz Xaver Süssmayer, around the 15th of August, 1791. Just as they were entering the coach, a grey-haired messenger arrived to enquire about the *Requiem*. Mozart was appalled. He excused himself on the grounds of the urgency of his journey to Prague, and promised to work on the *Requiem* as soon as the Coronation opera was completed. His feelings that autumn must have been very different from those that had inspired him in the golden September of 1787, for his thoughts were torn in three directions: *The Magic Flute, La Clemenza di Tito* and the *Requiem*.

By a superhuman effort Mozart forced himself to concentrate on the Coronation opera, and as soon as he entered the coach he began to draft out the various parts of the opera, so that he could hand it over to the copyists in Prague in a more or less finished state. The première was due in a few days. When they stopped to change horses, they dined and then withdrew to rest. Mozart and Süssmayer talked about the opera by candle light and Mozart continued writing until far into the night. The recitatives he entrusted to Süssmayer. In the morning he entered the coach in a high fever and arrived in Prague as one in a trance. His friends were shocked to see how wan and sad he looked, although from time to time he burst out into his usual boyish laughter. As always the Dušeks received Mozart at the Bertramka with open arms and there in the leafy stillness he finished *La Clemenza di Tito*. The next morning he hastened to the rehearsal at the Nostitz Theatre, driving through a Prague which was decked out for the Coronation and was gay with music, circus attractions and dancing.

Leopold II did not care for Mozart, if only because his brother Joseph liked him. He preferred the Italians. Salieri was in Prague with the court orchestra and so was Leopold Koželuh who lost no occasion of helping the suave Salieri to put obstacles in Mozart's way. Mozart would say of Salieri: "Honey-tongued, but a peppery heart." A harassing time now began for Mozart. What must his disappointment have been when on 6th September, at the première, the Empress, Maria Ludovica, declared that Mozart's opera was "porcheria tedesca" – (German swinishness). That was his reward for his titanic efforts, for all the beauty that came straight from his heart, in the belief that Prague would not disappoint him. But the people of

Prague never got to the theatre that evening. The entire Austrian court, ambassadors and guests from all over Germany, Italy, France, England and Spain were present. Mozart's real Prague public had to wait for the next performance.

Mozart was back in Vienna when news of the success of the opera reached him. The clarinet player Stadler informed him of it. Parts of it had to be repeated and Stadler wrote to him how the Prague audience—"Oh, Czech miracle!" as he called it—acclaimed it from the stalls and even from the orchestra pit. While still in Prague Mozart wrote for *The Magic Flute* the priests' chorus, *Isis and Osiris*, Papageno's songs and the second finale, as well as part of the overture and a concerto for clarinet which he left with Stadler. When Mozart left Prague that time he wept. He must have sensed that he would never again see his dear friends, never again hear the wild applause of an audience which understood him as did no other audience in the world.

## THE BELLS TOLL FOR MOZART

The news of Mozart's death in the night of 5th December, that reached Prague from Vienna on the 9th of December, 1791, flew through the city like a raven. None would believe it, so beloved was he. But after a time of profound sadness, the musicians of Prague went over to action. How they must have loved him, since within a very few days a *Requiem* which required a choir of 120 people was ready for performance. Mozart's Prague orchestra with its conductor, Josef Strobach, had cards printed for Mozart's funeral mass. The entire first page of the Prague newspapers was devoted to Mozart. On the 14th of December, solemn mass was celebrated in the Parish Church of St. Nicholas in the Malá Strana of Prague. All the bells in Prague were ringing. So great were the crowds that the huge church could not hold them and they overflowed on to the square outside. It is recorded that about three thousand people came to the funeral mass. Němeček wrote: "The sorrow for our darling was universal and unfeigned. In Vienna they honoured his memory in a dignified manner, but it was Prague that showed the most sincere sorrow, the warmest feeling. Never was there a more moving funeral mass. A choir of 120 singers, picked from among the best artists in Prague all of whom offered their services sadly and willingly—Josefa Dušek sang the soprano part—performed the masterly Rosetti *Requiem* under Strobach's baton so movingly, that it made the deepest impression on the assembled crowds." This was the first requiem for Mozart. Prague showed its love for him even after death. It opened its arms to his two orphans, Karl and Wolfgang (Franz Xaver), and cared for them lovingly for six years.

## PRAGUE REMAINS TRUE TO MOZART

Prague remained faithful in its love for the genius who had dedicated to it his *Don Giovanni* and it held his name in such high honour that any later composer who reaped success in Prague looked on it as a high light in his career. Hector Berlioz wrote with pride of this, and, speaking of the Czech people, he said: "I know no higher degree of musicianship." He was thrilled with the audience in which wide social strata were represented and he praised their "memory rich in musical impressions, capable of comparing works known and unknown, old and new, good and bad."

Mozart's works continued to meet with great response and to have a tremendous influence in the Czech lands. The entire Czech "awakening" period of the 19th century is permeated by the great beauty and deep humanity of the Master's legacy. Many Czech composers of that time and later (F. X. Dušek, J. A. Koželuh, V. J. Praupner, J. Křt. Kuchař, V. Mašek, J. Jelínek, the brothers Antonín & Pavel Vranický, J. T. Held, J. A. Vitásek, V. J. Tomášek, V. Jírovec, etc.), continued to spread Mozart's fame. To Bedřich Smetana Mozart was a great example, to Antonín Dvořák he was "the sun", the giver of untold warmth. The Mozart tradition became an inseparable and living part of Czech culture.

Prague led Czechoslovakia in preparations for a splendid celebration of the 200th anniversary of Mozart's birth, above all in the performance of almost all his works and of the compositions of his Czech forerunners and contemporaries, on the radio, at concert and opera halls; and lectures, exhibitions and publications were arranged with valuable contributions of literary works and paintings (memorial tablets in Prague and Brno, memorial medallions, postage stamps, post cards, etc.). The celebrations began with a Mozart week from the 22nd to the 29th of January, and reached their climax at the Prague Spring International Music Festival with an international conference of music experts on the life and work of W. A. Mozart attended by 40 outstanding musicologists from abroad and many Czech musicologists. On the eve of the opening of this conference, 25th May, the W. A. Mozart and Dušek Memorial at the Bertramka was unveiled.

## PRAGUE NEVER FAILED MOZART AND NEVER WILL

Few places in Prague are surrounded with such a halo of musical legends and romantic tales as the Bertramka, which lies in a delightful little valley in the Smíchov quarter. Schurig once wrote that "The Bertramka can be called Mozart's home, rather than the houses which he inhabited in Salzburg and Vienna." Josefa Dušek bought the Bertramka in 1784; three years later, in 1787, and again in 1791 this charming residence went down to history because of Mozart's visits. The Bertramka and its hostess offered Mozart a kindly refuge and warm hospitality at a time when his creative powers were being taxed to the full. The house was at that time somewhat different from the one which has been preserved to the present day. Presumably it was surrounded by a long, low balcony overgrown with grape vines and decorated by a high roof covered with sculpted tiles as was typical of buildings in the Prague of around 1700.

After the death of her husband, Mrs. Dušek sold the Bertramka in 1799. It passed into the hands of several owners until after an execution order had been served on the last owner, Mozart's admirer, Lambert Popelka, bought it in 1838. Popelka's son, Adolf, followed in the tradition of preserving the Bertramka as a Mozart memorial. Until then there are no written records nor any pictures which could throw light on the original design of the Bertramka. The first record of it dates from 1878, after a fire in January 1871 which changed both the inner and outer appearance of the residence. Happily, as though by a miracle, the fire did not touch that building which Mozart most probably inhabited. Not even the letter from Mozart's son, Karl, to Popelka contains anything from which it would be possible to reconstruct a picture of the interior or the exterior of the house as it was during Mozart's stay; a passage in it reads: "I remember every room and every nook and cranny of the garden." Only the contract of sale drawn up when Mrs. Dušek sold the Bertramka gives us some picture of the original interior "... with all fixtures and fittings, except the china, the paintings, the copper engravings, chandeliers and the attached bronze, on the small table in the cabinet and the two bookcases, everything as it stands..."

For the 200th Mozart anniversary celebrations, the Czechoslovak state spared neither effort nor expense to turn the Bertramka into a lasting and dignified memorial to this immortal genius. In the course of the work a number of interesting discoveries were made. It was ascertained, for instance, that where the fireplace stood in Mozart's bedroom, there had originally been a window, and that the room had been made considerably smaller by a wall, built probably after the fire. Everything was put back in its original state. All the objects which have any bearing on Mozart's stay and creative activities in Prague were assembled in five rooms. The Mozart and Dušek memorial at the Bertramka provides further proof of the fact that the slogan, "Prague never failed Mozart and never will" is as topical today as it was in 1928, when the famous Czech composer, Leoš Janáček, wrote these words in the visitor's book at the Bertramka.

# PLATES

## PHOTOGRAPHS BY:

Brok Jindřich, Prague.

Cultural Department of the Brno National Committee.

Ehm Josef, Prague.

Illek and Paul, Prague.

Konstantinová Taťána, Prague.

Krahulec Jan, Prague.

Mulač, Prague.

Dr. Novák Josef, Prague.

Renner Bedřich, Prague.

Dr. Smetana Robert, Olomouc.

State Administration of Cultural Monuments in Prague, J. Tuháček.

Tmej Zdeněk, Prague.

**WOLFGANG AMADEUS MOZART**
*(full name Johannes Chrystostomus Wolfgangus Theophilus), born 27th January, 1756, in Salzburg.*
Oil-painting by unknown artist, beginning of 19th century. Bertramka, Mozart and Dušek Memorial.

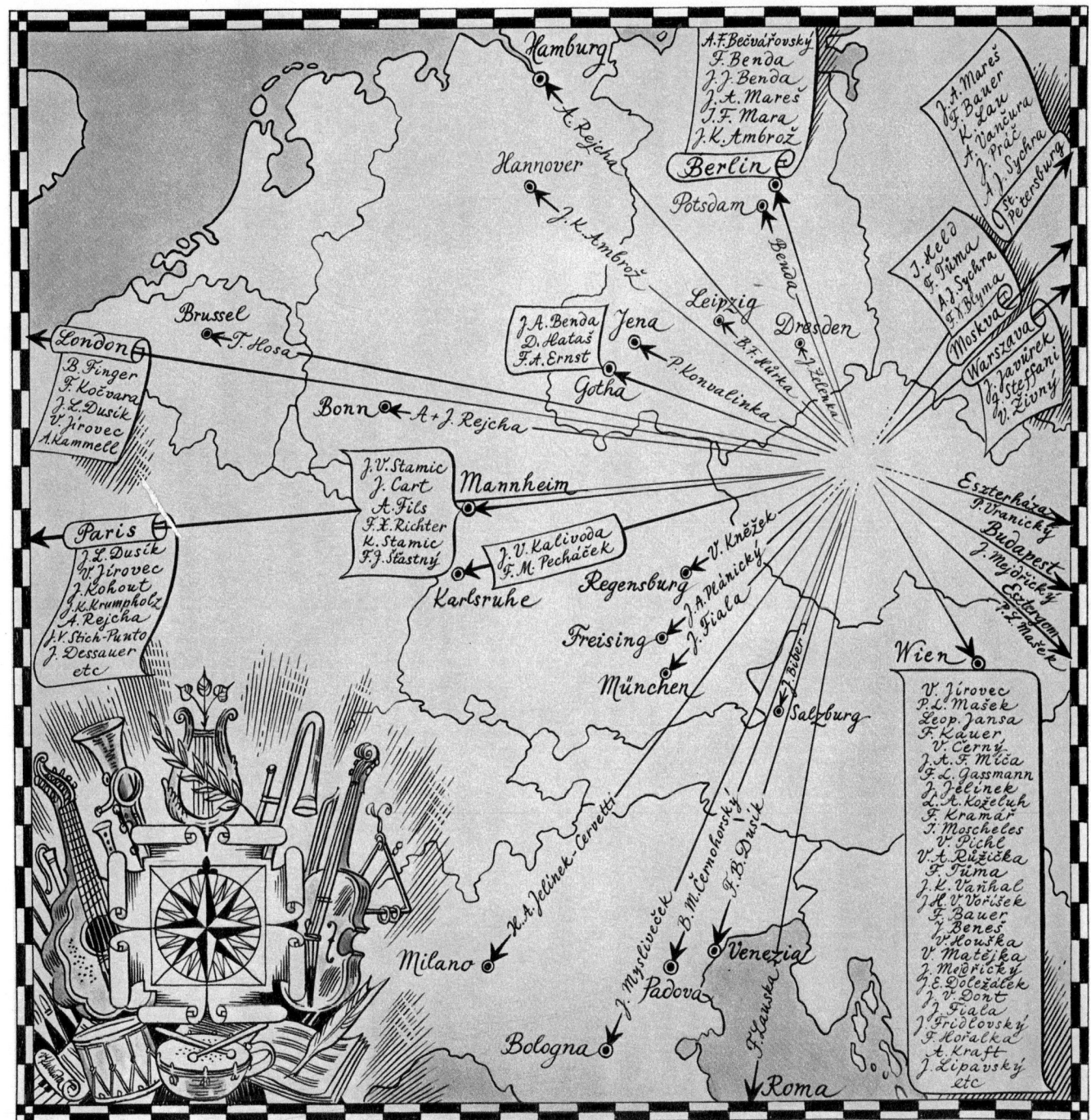

## BOHEMIA – THE CONSERVATOIRE OF EUROPE

*In the 18th century the Czech Lands boasted so many musicians that they fully earned the title of "Conservatoire of Europe", given them by Charles Burney. The fact that there were so many musicians, plus the social and religious conditions of the time, forced many to emigrate to various countries of the world.*

Coloured pen drawing by V. Kubašta. Bertramka, Mozart and Dušek Memorial.

JOSEF MYSLIVEČEK-VENATORINI

*known in Italy as "Il divino Boemo" (the divine Czech), famous composer*
*(1737–1781). Both Mozarts, father and son, were friends of Mysliveček.*
Engraving by A. Wiederhofer. Vienna, Gesellschaft der Musikfreunde.

FRANTIŠEK TŮMA

*composer of sacred music, a pupil of Bohuslav Černohorský (1704–1774).*
*His orchestral suites and chamber music were in line with the new homo-*
*phonic style. Mozart knew his works and studied them thoroughly.*
Engraving by J. Balzer, after A. Hickel.

### JIŘÍ ANTONÍN BENDA

*the founder of the melodrama (1722–1795). Mozart speaks enthusiastically*
*of Benda's works in a letter to his father, dated November 12th, 1778: "…what*
*I saw was Medea by Benda; he also wrote Ariadne on Naxos… I liked*
*both these works so much that I carry them about with me."*

**BENDA'S MANUSCRIPT**
*in which he speaks of his melodramas.*
Prague, Department of Literature, National Museum.

JAN ANTONÍN KOŽELUH

*director of the choir at the Church of the Crusaders in Prague, later
choirmaster at St. Vitus's Cathedral; composer (1738–1814). There
is a marked resemblance to Mozart's music in his concerto for oboe.*

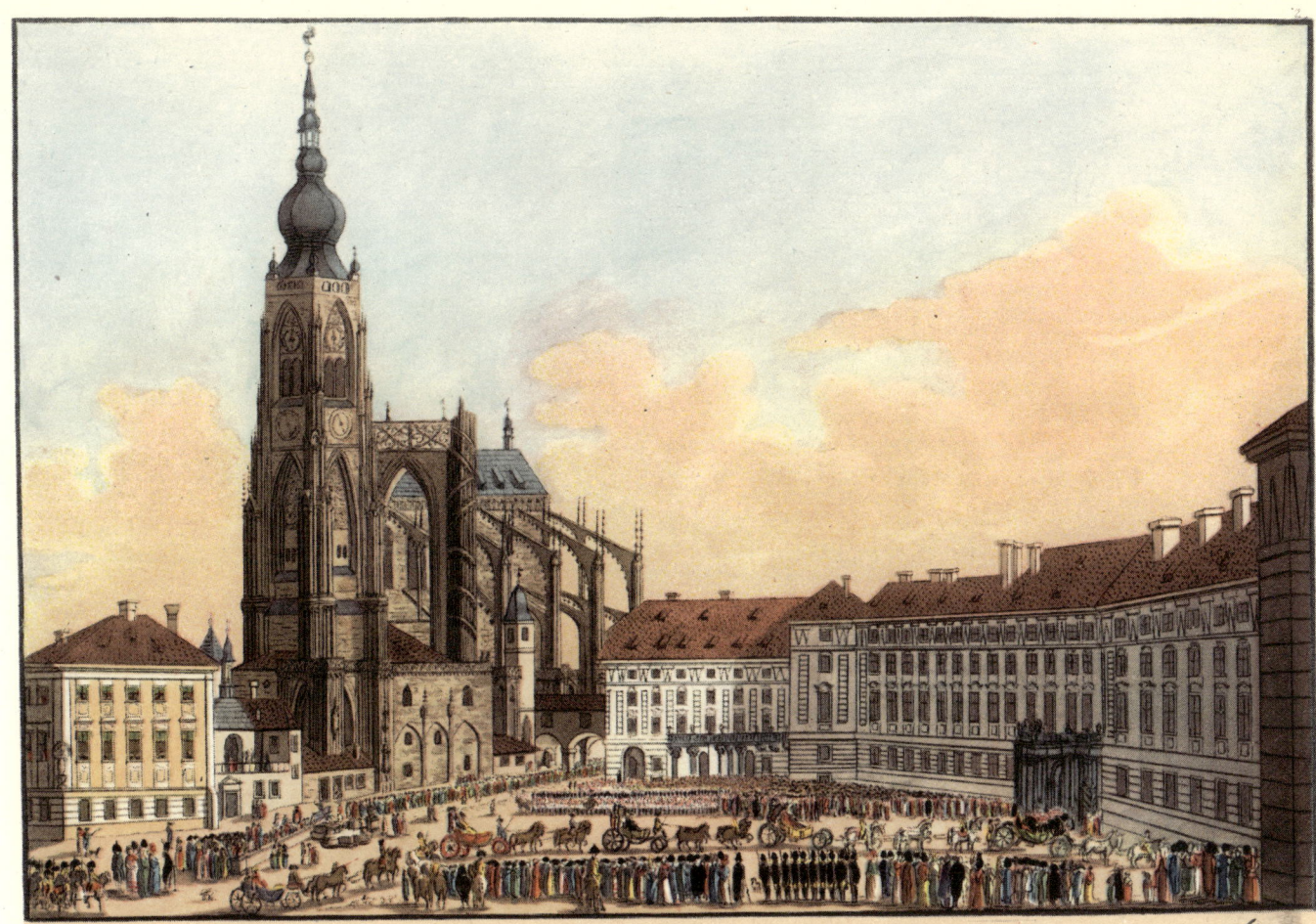

*Prospect der K.K. Residenz nebst der Dom Kirche in Prag wie solcher zwishen Mittag und Abend gegen Mitternacht und Morgen anzusehen ist. Nebst der Ankunft Seiner Königl. Hoheiten der Erz-Herzogin Mariane in Prag den 17 July Anno 1793.*

## ST. VITUS'S CATHEDRAL IN PRAGUE
*the scene of action of many outstanding Czech musicians and composers. During Mozart's time, F. X. Brixi, J. A. Koželuh, J. Vencl and J. N. Vitásek officiated there.*
Engraving by J. Balzer after L. Pauckert.

## MOZART'S FAMILY

*His father, Leopold Mozart (1719–1787), violinist, composer and second conductor at the archiepiscopal seat at Salzburg, Wolfgang Amadeus and Wolfgang's sister Maria Anna (1751–1829), who accompanied her brother on his first concert tours. In the framed picture is the mother of Wolfgang, Anna Maria Mozart, née Pertl.*

Lithograph from the original in the Salzburg Museum by G. N. della Croce, 1780; Bertramka, Mozart and Dušek Memorial.

### JAN VÁCLAV STICH

*known also as Punto (1746–1803). Excellent French Horn player and composer. Mozart wrote of him on 5th April, 1781: "Punto bläst magnifique." Mozart also showed his admiration of Punto's playing by writing a part for the French Horn in his Sinfonia Concertante (K. V. 297b).*

Engraving by S. C. Miger after C. N. Cochet.

### JAN VAŇHAL

*composer (1739–1813). Violoncellist in the quartet in which Mozart played the viola. In a letter to his father dated 24th October, 1777, Mozart writes from Augsburg that he played Vaňhal's concerto in B ♮ with great success.*

THEATRE IN THE KOTCE LANE
*in Prague Old Town. Italian opera was greatly favoured here at one time and Bondini, the charming Italian singer, sang here; later as Zerlina she sang in Don Giovanni.*
Engraving by J. Berka.

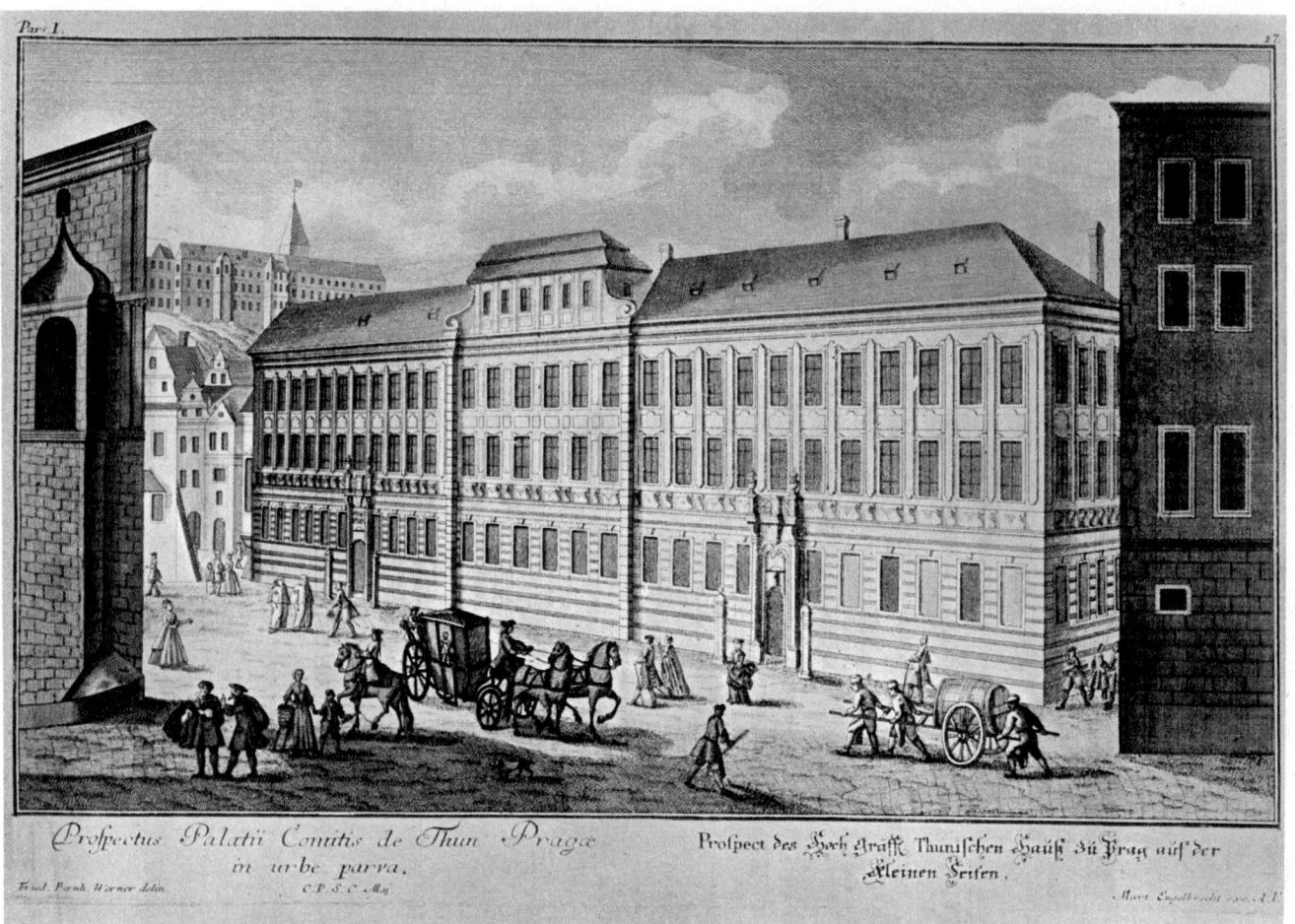

Prospectus Palatii Comitis de Thun Pragæ
in urbe parva.
C. P. S. C. May.

Prospect des Hoch Gräffl Thunischen Hauß zu Prag auff der
Kleinen Seiten.

Fried. Bernh. Werner delin.

Mart Engelbrecht excud. A. V.

THUN THEATRE
*in Malá Strana on Five Churches Square; it was burnt down in 1794.*
Etching by M. Engelbrecht after F. B. Werner.

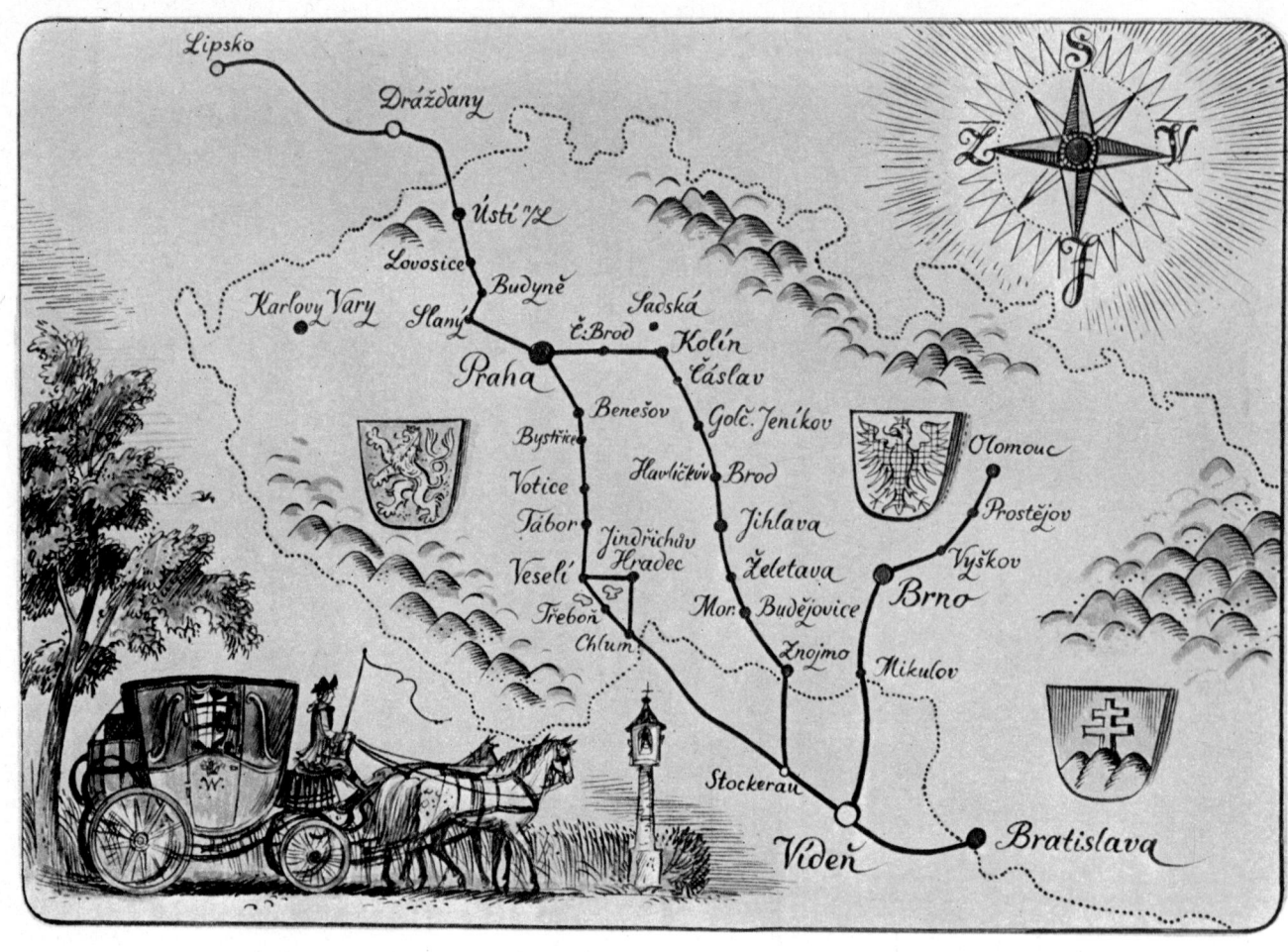

**MOZART'S TRAVELS**
*in Bohemia, Moravia and Slovakia.*
Tinted pen drawing by V. Kubašta. Bertramka, Mozart and
Dušek Memorial.

**BRATISLAVA**

*(formerly Pressburg), capital of Slovakia in the baroque period. In 1762 Mozart, then six years old, went to Pressburg on the invitation of Baron L. Amadé and the Counts of Pálffy, where he gave a concert which was most successful.*

Engraving by J. C. Liopold after F. B. Werner. Bratislava, Municipal Museum.

MOZART IN GALA DRESS
*presented to him by Maria Theresa. Mozart arrived in Pressburg on the invitation
of Baron L. Amadé and the Counts of Pálffy.*

THE CHILD MOZART AT THE PIANO
*Czech folk painting on glass, beginning of the 19th century.*
Bertramka, Mozart and Dušek Memorial.

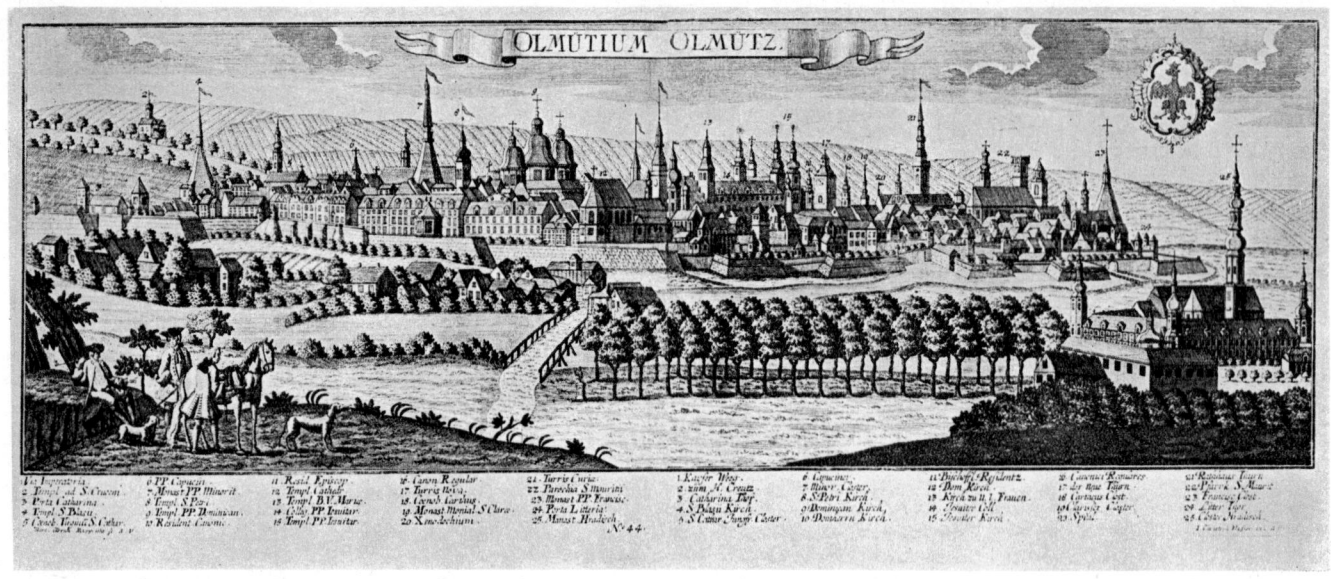

OLOMOUC IN THE 18TH CENTURY

*In 1767 Leopold Mozart fled with his family before the small-pox in Vienna to Olomouc, where he arrived on the 26th October. He stayed first at the inn "U černého orla" (The Black Eagle), later at the home of the Dean of the Chapter, Podstatsky-Lichtenstein.*

Print by Haffner after an engraving by Rupprecht.

MOZART 11 YEARS OLD

Oil-painting by J. van der Smissen. Salzburg, Internationale Stiftung
Mozarteum.

### THE HOUSE OF THE DEAN OF THE CHAPTER IN OLOMOUC

*with baroque chapel, St. Barbara (originally a Romanesque fortress rotunda). Right fore-ground St. Anne's Chapel (Patron Saint of the Archbishops of Olomouc) and part of the façade of St. Wenceslas's Cathedral (founded in 1109) for which Ludwig van Beethoven wrote his Missa solemnis.*

### LEOPOLD MOZART

*"Te Deum laudamus! Little Wolfgang has happily survived the small-
pox! And where? — in Olomouc!" writes Mozart's father from Olomouc on November 10th, 1767.*

Prague shadow print. Bertramka, Mozart and Dušek Memorial.

*Brünn, Ansicht von der Südseite.*

VIEW OF BRNO FROM SOUTH
18th century engraving. Prague, Museum of National Literature.

### TAVERN HOUSE IN THE VEGETABLE MARKET

*in Brno where on the return journey from Olomouc to Vienna on 30th December, 1767, Mozart and his sister gave a concert. The musicians of the T. A. Fischer Brno orchestra accompanied the young artists.*

**MOZART MEMORIAL PLAQUE**
*on the Schrattenbach House in Koblížná Street in Brno, designed by J. T. Fischer, with the inscription, "W. A. Mozart lived here in December 1767 and January 1768."*

COUNT SCHRATTENBACH'S HOUSE
*in Kobližná Street, Brno, where the Mozarts lived in the second half of December
1767 and the beginning of January 1768.*

**FRANTIŠEK ANTONÍN, COUNT NOSTITZ-RINEK**

*Crown Sheriff and President of the Provincial Government in Bohemia. He conceived the idea of building a fitting theatre in Prague on the pattern of theatres in foreign cities. In spite of the resistance of the municipal council and the owners of the adjoining houses the foundation stone was laid on 7th June, 1781.*

Oil-painting by unknown artist. Bertramka, Mozart and Dušek Memorial.

*Gustav desf. dapres la nature et grave.*

*Der Kleinseitner Platz mit der Nikolaus Kirche.*

CHURCH OF ST. NICHOLAS
*in the Malá Strana where the solemn mass was celebrated for Mozart on December*
*14th, 1791.*
Engraving by Gustav.

# LE NOZZE DI FIGARO,

O SIA

## LA FOLLE GIORNATA.

COMEDIA PER MUSICA

TRATTA DAL FRANCESE

IN QUATTRO ATTI.

DA RAPPRESENTARSI

Nei Teatri di Praga
l'Anno 1786.

Preſo Giuſeppe Emanuele Diesbach.

LIBRETTO OF THE MARRIAGE OF FIGARO
*printed in Prague in 1786.*
Prague, Music Department of the National Museum.

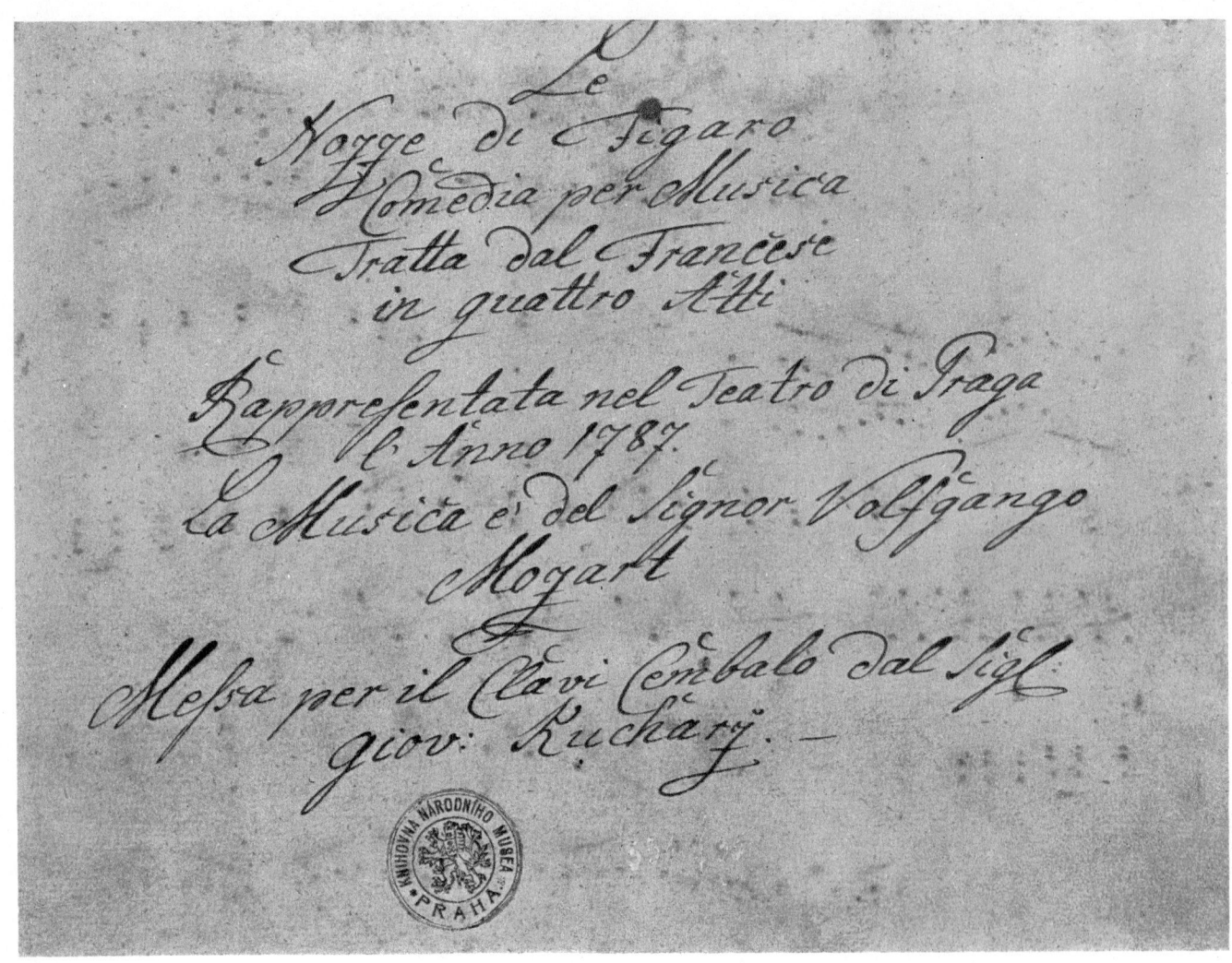

**PIANO SCORE OF THE MARRIAGE OF FIGARO**

*by Jan Křtitel Kuchař, organist at St. Jindřich's and at Strahov, and director of the Italian opera in Prague. Among the connoisseurs and admirers of Mozart's music Kuchař's position is an honourable one. He was an outstanding composer and soloist and arranged piano scores of other operas by Mozart as well.*

Prague, Music Department of National Museum.

THE FRENCH GATE AT VYŠEHRAD
*through which the road from Vienna to Prague led.*
Lithograph by J. Vopálenský. Bertramka, Mozart and Dušek Memorial.

MOZART

*arrived in Prague for the first time on January 11th, 1787, in answer
to the wishes of his Prague friends.*

Contemporary engraving by J. G. Mansfeld after Posche. Prague,
Music Department of National Museum.

Leop. Peuckert del.

Ansicht der Stadt **PRAG** von dem Stift Strahof. ☀ Vue de la Ville de **PRAGUE** prise du Couvent de Strahof.

à Prague chez Marco Berra Marché aux Estampes.

**PRAGUE—MOZART'S CITY**
Coloured etching by L. Peuckert.

1787.  Nro. 4.

von Schönfeldsche

## k. k. Prager Oberpostamtszeitung.

Gestern Abends kam unser große und geliebte Tonkünstler Hr. Mozard aus Wien hier an. Wir zweifeln nicht, daß Herr Bondini diesem Manne zu Ehren die Hochzeit des Figaro, dieß bellebte Werk seines musikalischen Genies, aufführen lassen werde, und unser rühmlich bekanntes Orchester wird sodann nicht ermangeln neue Beweise seiner Kunst zu geben, und die geschmackvollen Bewohner Prags werden sich gewiß, ohngeacht sie das Stück schon oft gehört haben, sehr zahlreich einfinden. Wir wünschten auch Herrn Mozards Spiel selbst bewundern zu können.

ANNOUNCEMENT IN THE PRAGUE POST NEWSPAPER
*on 12th January, 1787, of Mozart's arrival in Prague.*
Prague, Museum of National Literature.

*Gemahlt von Norb. Grund.*                    *Gestochen von Johann Balzer.*

*Die Cassation.*

### CZECH CHAMBER ORCHESTRA IN 18TH CENTURY
*At Count Thun's house Mozart heard for the first time a Czech aristocratic chamber orchestra.*
*Mozart's praise in his letter to G. von Jacquin, dated 15th January, 1787, speaks eloquently of the*
*high artistic level of the Prague musicians of the time.*
Etching by J. Balzer after N. Grund. Prague, privately owned.

### PALACE OF JAN JOSEF, COUNT THUN
*in the Malá Strana in Thun Street where Mozart stayed on arrival.*

JOSEPHUS MALABAILA COMES DE CANAL.

## JOSEF EMANUEL, COUNT CANAL OF MALABAIL

*Grand Master of the Mason's Lodge in Prague, with whom Mozart attended the so-called Bretfeld Ball on his arrival. "...I watched with pleasure how all those people skipped and turned to the music ital. of my Figaro, arranged for contre-dances and tedeschi; the talk was of nothing else but Figaro; they play, blow, sing and whistle Figaro. Nobody goes to any opera but Figaro and again Figaro," wrote Mozart to Gottfried von Jacquin on January 15th, 1787.*

INVITATION (ADMISSION CARD) TO THE "CANAL" DANCES
*in the English garden of Count Canal, which Mozart visited during his stay
in Prague.*
Prague Museum.

THE CLEMENTINUM LIBRARY
*in Prague Old Town; opposite the Church of the Crusaders with the*
*red star, and in the background the Palace of Count Pachta.*
Engraving by V. Morstadt. Prague, National Gallery.

Gemalt von gebh. Kneipp.    Gestochen von I. Balzer.

*Raphael Ungar*
*erster K.K.*
*Bibliothekar zu Prag.*

FR. RAFAEL UNGAR

*distinguished figure of the "Enlightenment" movement, director of*
*the Clementinum library. He accompanied Mozart through the*
*library on the second day after the latter's arrival in Prague.*

Engraving by J. Balzer after G. Kneipp.

*Collegium Nobilium Virginum in Nova urbe Pragensi, prope forum pecuarium situm.*

*Das Adeliche Frauen Stisst auf der Neu Stadt Prag am Vich marckt gelegen.*

F. B. Werner delin.     Cum Priv. Sac. Cæs. Maj.     I. G. Ringle fecit.     Mart. Engelbrecht excud. A.V.

LADIES' COLLEGE
*in Prague New Town.*
Engraving by M. Engelbrecht, after F. B. Werner. Bertramka,
Mozart and Dušek Memorial.

THE PIANO
*on which Mozart played at the Ladies' College in January 1787.*
Bertramka, Mozart and Dušek Memorial.

JAN COUNT PACHTA
Oil-painting by Franz von Fahrenschon. Prague, privately owned.

HOUSE OF MOZART'S PATRON, JAN COUNT PACHTA
*in the Old Town. As early as 1777 Mysliveček made an attempt to introduce*
*Mozart to him.*
Watercolour by V. Kubašta.

**"6 TEDESCHI" (SIX GERMAN DANCES)**
*composed by Mozart during his first stay in Prague (K. V. 509).*
Berlin, National Library.

**POEM IN HONOUR**

*of the Pasquale Bondini's Italian Theatre Society by whom Italian opera was*
*cultivated in Prague. This society was active at the Thun theatre in 1781 and*
*from 1784 at the Nostitz Theatre.*

Prague, Museum of National Literature.

*Giov. Paisiello*

**GIOVANNI PAISIELLO**

*Italian operatic composer (1740–1816). Mozart attended the Prague perform-ance of his opera Le gare generose at the Nostitz Theatre on 13th January, 1787.*

W. A. MOZART

*Medallion from the estate of F. X. Němeček the younger.*
Bertramka, Mozart and Dušek Memorial.

**"NOVÁ HOSPODA" – NEW INN**
*now "U zlatého anděla" – the Golden Angel – on the corner of Celetná and Rybná Streets in Prague
Old Town, to which Mozart moved from the Thun Palace.*
Coloured lithograph by V. Kubašta.

## JOSEF HAISLER

*Prague harp player, also known as "Pigtail". Legend has it that Mozart played*
*him a theme at the "New Inn" on which Haisler improvised variations.*
Lithograph after S. Pfalz, 1834. Prague, Music Department of the National
Museum.

MANOR IN JINDŘICHŮV HRADEC
*which Mozart visited on his second visit to Prague in September 1787.*

TITLE PAGE OF THE CONTRE-DANCES
*composed by Mozart for Jan Rudolf, Count Černín, in Jindřichův Hradec.*
Manor archives, Jindřichův Hradec.

### THE COAL MARKET

*in Prague Old Town at the time of Mozart's stay. Right: the inn "U tři zlatých lvů" (The Three Golden Lions), where Mozart stayed for only a short time before moving to the Bertramka in order to complete Don Giovanni, the opera which he had promised to the people of Prague. Left: the "Platýz House" in which Mozart's librettist Lorenzo da Ponte stayed.*
Coloured pen drawing by V. Kubašta.

### W. A. MOZART

*Marble relief by Taťana Konstantinova on the house "U tří zlatých lvů", unveiled on May 29th, 1956.*

LORENZO DA PONTE
*poet and adventurer (1749–1838). Author of the librettos for Mozart's operas The Marriage of Figaro, Don Giovanni and Cosi fan Tutte.*

*IIᵗᵉ Ansicht der Prager Brücke.* ✳ *IIᵐᵉ Vue du Pont de la Ville de Prague.*

a Prague chez Marco Berra March. d. des Estampes.

PRAGUE, WITH A VIEW OF THE CHARLES BRIDGE
*which Mozart often passed over on his way to the Bertramka.*
Engraving by J. Balzer after Scotti de Cassano. Prague, National Gallery.

# IL
# DISSOLUTO
## PUNITO.
### O SIA
## IL D. GIOVANNI.

## DRAMMA GIOCOSO
### IN DUE ATTI.

DA RAPPRESENTARSI

NEL TEATRO DI PRAGA L' ANNO 1787.

IN PRAGA.

*di Schœnfeld.*

FIRST EDITION OF THE LIBRETTO OF
DON GIOVANNI
*published in Prague, 1787.*
Prague, University Library.

INTERIOR OF THE "U TEMPLU" INN

*with an inscription on the wall which reads "Hier hat Mozart gegessen, getrunken und componiert, w. z. B. Schnitzel, Wein u. Don Juan 1787"; ("Here Mozart ate, drank and composed, e. g. 'schnitzel' wine and Don Giovanni, 1787").*

Oil-painting by J. Minařík, 1911. Prague, Music Department of National Museum.

"U TEMPLU" INN

*later re-named "Mozartův sklípek" (The Mozart Cellar). It stood on the site of No. 7, Temple Street in Prague Old town. (It was pulled down in 1911.)*

Engraving by K. Dostál.

MOZART'S LETTER FROM PRAGUE, *15th October, 1787, to Gottfried von Jacquin in which he explains why the première of Don Giovanni was twice postponed. It was originally fixed for the 14th October but was first postponed to the 24th October, the performers being insufficiently prepared and later — because one of the singers had fallen ill — to the 29th October.*

Jindřichův Hradec, Manor archives.

MOZART.

W. A. MOZART

Engraving by J. Blaschke. Prague, Music Department of the
National Museum.

*Die Theinkirche mit dem Fürst. Kinskischen Palais*
*auf dem Altstädter Ring gegen Mitternacht.*

**OLD TOWN SQUARE IN PRAGUE**
*In front of the Church of Our Lady is the house in which the composer and choirmaster Václav Josef Praupner lived*
*(1744–1807). Mozart went to see him to discuss the performance of Don Giovanni.*
Engraving by V. Morstadt. Prague, National Gallery.

## SERENADE

*from the second act of Don Giovanni, composed in Prague. This score, from which Mozart conducted the opera four times in Prague, was sold by his widow to the publisher, André. It was offered to the Imperial Library in Vienna without success. Finally the famous singer, Viardot-Garcia, bought it and left it in her will to the Paris Conservatoire.*

Altera nunc rerum facies, me quero, nec adsum:
Non sum qui fueram non putor esse: fui.

GIACOMO CASANOVA
*adventurer and writer (1725–1798), proposed a text for the sextet in Don Gio-*
*vanni (Act II).*
Engraving by J. Berka, Duchcov, Municipal Museum.

PART OF THE MANUSCRIPT PROPOSED BY CASANOVA
Mnichovo Hradiště, State Agricultural Archives.

Il solo Don Giovanni
M'astrinse a mascherarmi
Egli di tanti affanni
E l'unica cagion.
Io merito perdon.
Colpevole non son
La colpa è tutta quanta
Di quel femineo volto
Che l'anima gl'incanta
E gl'incatena il cor.
O volto seduttor!
Sorgente di dolor!

~~Il povere Leporino~~
Lasciate andar in pace
Un povero innocente
Non sono contumace
Offender vi non so
E ve lo proverò
Fu lui che si poffiò
Di prese i panni miei
Per bastonar Masetto
Con donna Elvira io fei
Il solo mio dover
~~gl'falsò il suo voler~~
Quel che vi dico e ver

~~Lasciatemi goder~~
~~stringe l'uno colorito~~
Sol
~~Lasciate Don Giovanni~~
~~Fuoche......~~

~~Lasciatemi scapar~~
~~Sol qui marito......~~
vostro degno
~~... Il solo don Giovanni~~
Ha a punir l'indegno
Lasciatemi scapar ———— Peggio

MOZART'S LETTER FROM PRAGUE *to Gottfried von Jacquin, dated 4th November, 1787, in which he describes his joy at the successful première of Don Giovanni. "On October 29th my opera, Don Giovanni, was performed for the first time with tremendous success... I only wish that my good friends (particularly Bridi and you) could spend just one evening here and share in my joy!"*

Vienna, National Library.

1787.        Nro. 88.

von Schönfeldsche

k. k. Prager Oberpostamtszeitung.

Montags den 29ten wurde von der italienischen Operngesellschaft die mit Sehnsucht erwartete Oper des Meisters Mozard Don Giovani, oder das steinerne Gastmahl gegeben. Kenner und Tonkünstler sagen, daß zu Prag ihres Gleichen noch nicht aufgeführt worden. Hr. Mozard dirigirte selbst, u. als er ins Orchester trat, wurde ihm ein dreymaliger Jubel gegeben, welches auch bey seinem Austritte aus demselben geschah. Die Oper ist übrigens äußerst schwer zu exequiren, und jeder bewundert dem ungeachtet die gute Vorstellung derselben nach so kurzer Studierzeit. Alles, Theater und Orchester bot seine Kräften auf, Mozarden zum Danke mit guter Exequirung zu belohnen. Es werden auch sehr viele Kosten durch mehrere Chöre und Dekorazion erfordert, welches alles Herr Guardasoni glänzend hergestellt hat. Die außerordentliche Menge Zuschauer bürgen für den allgemeinen Beyfall.

A NEWS ITEM ABOUT THE SUCCESSFUL
PREMIÈRE OF DON GIOVANNI
*in the Prague Post Newspaper of November 3rd, 1787.*
Prague, Museum of National Literature.

*Prospect von dem Altstädter National-Theater in Prag, wie solches von Abend gegen Morgen anzusehen ist.*

*zu finden bey Johann Balzer in Prag.*

**THE NOSTITZ THEATRE**

*with a view of its surroundings; this was the scene of the première of the opera Don Giovanni*
*(October 29th, 1787) and Mozart's triumph.*

Coloured etching by L. Peuckert.

JOSEPHUS II. ROM: IMPERATOR SEMPER AUGUSTUS
ET CONREGENS REGNORUM.

## THE EMPEROR JOSEPH II

*(1741–1790) said of Don Giovanni: "This is a heavenly opera; it is perhaps*
*even more beautiful than Figaro, but it is not food for my Viennese." Da Ponte*
*related this to Mozart who answered: "Let's give them time to chew it over."*

Engraving by J. Balzer, Prague, National Gallery.

ANNOUNCEMENT OF THE PERFORMANCE OF DON GIOVANNI
*23rd September, 1788. This is the oldest bill announcing the opera which has been preserved in Prague.*
Prague, Music Department of the National Museum.

THE OLDEST KNOWN DÉCOR FOR DON GIOVANNI
*for the Deutsche Schaubühne in Prague, beginning of the 19th century.*
Original design for the engraver by L. Peuckert. Prague, privately owned.

Saengerin Bondini als
Zerline.

Catarina Micelli als
Donna Elvira.

Saenger L. Basso als
Leporello.

Saengerin Saporiti als
Donna Anna.

THE FIRST PERFORMERS OF DON GIOVANNI
*Silhouettes from a group marking the première.*
Bertramka, Mozart and Dušek Memorial. From the Prague Museum.

*Direc. Lange und Frau.*

**DIRECTOR AND MRS. LANGE**
*Coloured silhouette from a group marking the première of Don Giovanni.*
Bertramka, Mozart and Dušek Memorial. From the Prague Museum.

CONJECTURAL BILL FOR THE PREMIÈRE OF DON GIOVANNI
*Probably no bill was printed to announce the première of Don Giovanni. One was published
by the German Theatre in Prague for the one-hundredth performance of the opera in 1887.*
Bertramka, Mozart and Dušek Memorial.

CONCERT ARIA "BELLA MIA FIAMMA, ADDIO!"
*(K. V. 528) dedicated to Josefa Dušek. It was written on 3rd November, 1787, at the Bertramka.*
Berlin, State Library.

MOZART PLAYING THE PIANO AT THE DUŠEKS'
*Coloured silhouette from a group marking the première of Don Giovanni.*
Bertramka, Mozart and Dušek Memorial.

### THE ORGAN

*in the carved choir of the Church of St. Mary, Strahov, from the year 1727, which
Mozart played during a visit to the church; it was rebuilt in 1784.*

**NORBERT IGNÁC LOEHMANN**
*noted down a fragment of Mozart's improvisations; this was preserved*
*as a Fantasy for organ (K. V. 528a).*
Prague, Music Department of the National Museum.

Gustav del.                                                                    Gr. fol Berka.

*Das Præmonstratenser Kloster Strahof gegen Mitternacht.*

*Verlegt bey Franz Zimmer & Sohn in Prag.*

### PREMONSTRATENSIAN MONASTERY, STRAHOV

*with the Church of Our Lady which Mozart visited in mid-November 1787 with Josefa Dušek. After going over the church Mozart expressed a wish to hear the famous organ which had been renovated shortly before. A member of the order, Loehmann, played for Mozart. Mozart then entered the choir and himself improvised for some time.*

Engraving by J. Berka after Gustav.

W. A. MOZART, JOSEPH HAYDN AND CONSTANZE
MOZART
*Nineteenth century painting on glass. Private collection.*

"U ZLATÉHO JEDNOROŽCE" INN

*(The Golden Unicorn) on the Malá Strana in Lázeňská Street, with a memorial plaque to Ludwig van Beethoven who lived there during his visit to Prague in 1796. Here Mozart spent the night when he arrived in Prague with his patron, Prince Karl Lichnovsky, on 10th April, 1789.*

*Peter Leopold II.*
*König von Ungarn, Böhmen und Gallizien &. &*

THE EMPEROR LEOPOLD II

*(1747–1792). About the middle of August, 1791, the Czech Estates requested Mozart*
*to write an opera – La Clemenza di Tito on a text by Metastasio.*
Coloured etching by L. Marek. Bertramka, Mozart and Dušek Memorial.

LA CLEMENZA

DI TITO,

DRAMMA SERIO PER MUSICA

IN DUE ATTI

DA RAPPRESENTARSI

NEL TEATRO NAZIONALE

DI PRAGA

NEL SETTEMBRE 1791.

IN OCCASIONE DI SOLLENIZZARE

IL GIORNO DELL' INCORONAZIONE

DI SUA

MAESTA L'IMPERATORE

LEOPOLDO II.

FIRST EDITION OF THE LIBRETTO OF
LA CLEMENZA DI TITO
*published in Prague in 1791.*
Prague, National Museum Library.

PIETRO METASTASIO

*Famous librettist of the 18th century. His libretto of 1734 was revised for Mozart by the
Saxon court poet Caterino Mazzola.*

Engraving by Bollinger, after Steiner.

ADMISSION CARD FOR THE ESTATES BALL
*in the Nostitz Theatre, organised in September 1791 in honour of*
*the Coronation. It is made out for Countess A. Sternberg and the*
*illustration on it of the Nostitz Theatre is the oldest one known.*
Prague Museum.

PROSPECT

*Des neü in Prag errichteten=böhmish=ständishen Saales beÿ der Krönungs Feÿer* LEOPOLD *des* II.ten
*und* MARIA LOUISE *K: K: Majestäten. año 1791.*

*Angegeben und im Werk ausgeführt durch J. Quirin Jahn.*          *Gezeichnet von J. A. Brößig Archit: und Mahler.*

*Verlegt beÿ Johann Balzer in Prag.*

ESTATES BALL

*in honour of the Coronation of Leopold II; it was held in a building added solely for this purpose
to the Nostitz Theatre.*

Colour etching by J. Q. Jahn. Prague, privately owned.

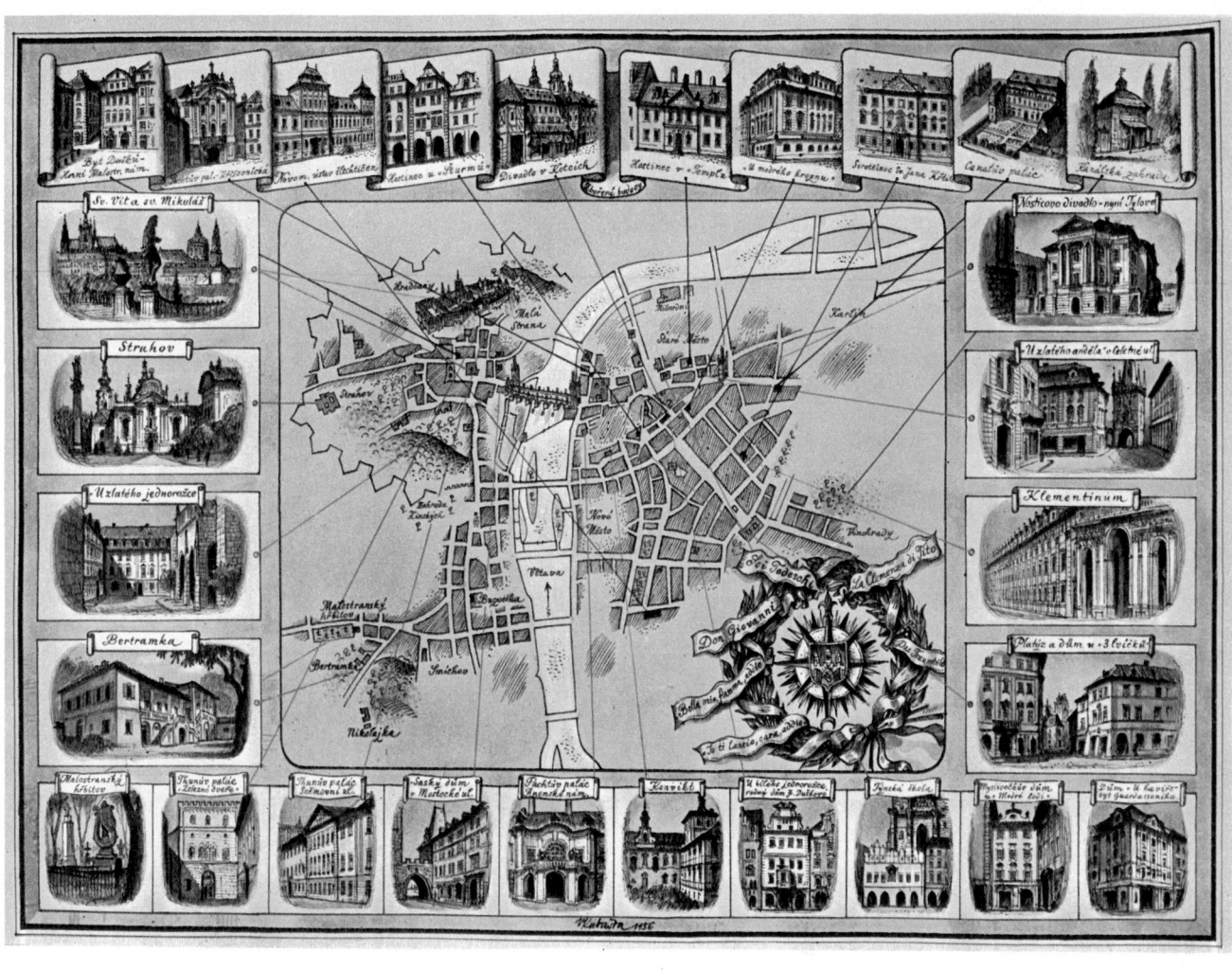

MOZART'S HAUNTS IN PRAGUE

Coloured pen drawing by V. Kubašta. Bertramka, Mozart and Dušek Memorial.

## HOLOGRAPH COPY OF CANTATA

*which L. Koželuh wrote on the occasion of the Coronation of Leopold II. It was performed on 12th September, 1791, during popular celebrations organised by the Czech Estates.*

Prague, State Central Archives.

Etching by E. E. Böhm. Vienna, Court Library.

## LEOPOLD KOŽELUH

*Composer and cousin of J. A. Koželuh (1752–1818). According to Němeček, Koželuh and Mozart once met at a party at which Haydn's string quartet was performed. After a particularly audacious passage, Koželuh remarked to Mozart: "I wouldn't have written it like that!", whereupon Mozart replied: "Nor would I, but do you know why? Because neither I nor you would have thought of it!" The story goes that since then Koželuh bore Mozart a grudge.*

Lithograph by E. E. Böhm. Vienna, Court Library.

HOLOGRAPH COPY OF CONCERT ARIA IO TI LASCIO, O CARA, ADDIO
*(K. V. 621a) which Mozart composed before leaving Prague.*
Vienna, privately owned.

**PRAGUE MUSICIANS**

Coloured etching from beginning of 19th century. Prague, Music Department of the National Museum.

### MOZART LEAVES PRAGUE FOR THE LAST TIME
*Ill, and disgusted at the failure of his opera La Clemenza di Tito, Mozart leaves Prague around the middle of September 1791 with a growing conviction that he will never again see his beloved city.*
Engraving by K. Dostál.

## MOZART

*died in Vienna, a broken man, on 5th December, 1791. He was buried in a mass grave with the poorest of the poor and as the grave was not marked it is not known to this day where he lies buried. Thus Mozart's perishable remains have mingled with the soil and disappeared for all time, while the splendid works of his immortal genius shine forth untarnished.*

Etching by K. Dostál.

Das ständ. Theater mit dem Universitäts oder Carolingebäude.
—— gegen Mitternacht. ——
Verlegt bev Franz Zimmer & Sohn in Prag.

**NOSTITZ NATIONAL THEATRE**

*in the Fruit Market in Prague Old Town, dedicated to "The Homeland and the Muses";*
*solemnly inaugurated on Easter Monday 1783 with Lessing's drama, Emilia Galotti.*
Engraving by J. Berka after Gustav. Bertramka, Mozart and Dušek Memorial.

MOZART'S GOLDEN FOB WATCH

*Mozart is supposed to have received this watch from the Czech musician, Gothard Pokorný (1733–1802) according to a story that is traditional in the family.*

### KONVIKT HALL

*in the Old Town where on the 7th of February, 1794, a memorial concert was held, attended by Mozart's widow and his son Karl. The programme consisted of a number of Mozart's works played by the Nostitz Theatre orchestra with Josefa Dušek as soloist.*

### CONSTANZE MOZART

*for whose benefit František, Count Sternberg, arranged a musical celebration on 13th January, 1792, in the Nostitz Theatre.*

Oil-painting by H. Hansen, 1802. Salzburg, Internationale Stiftung Mozarteum.

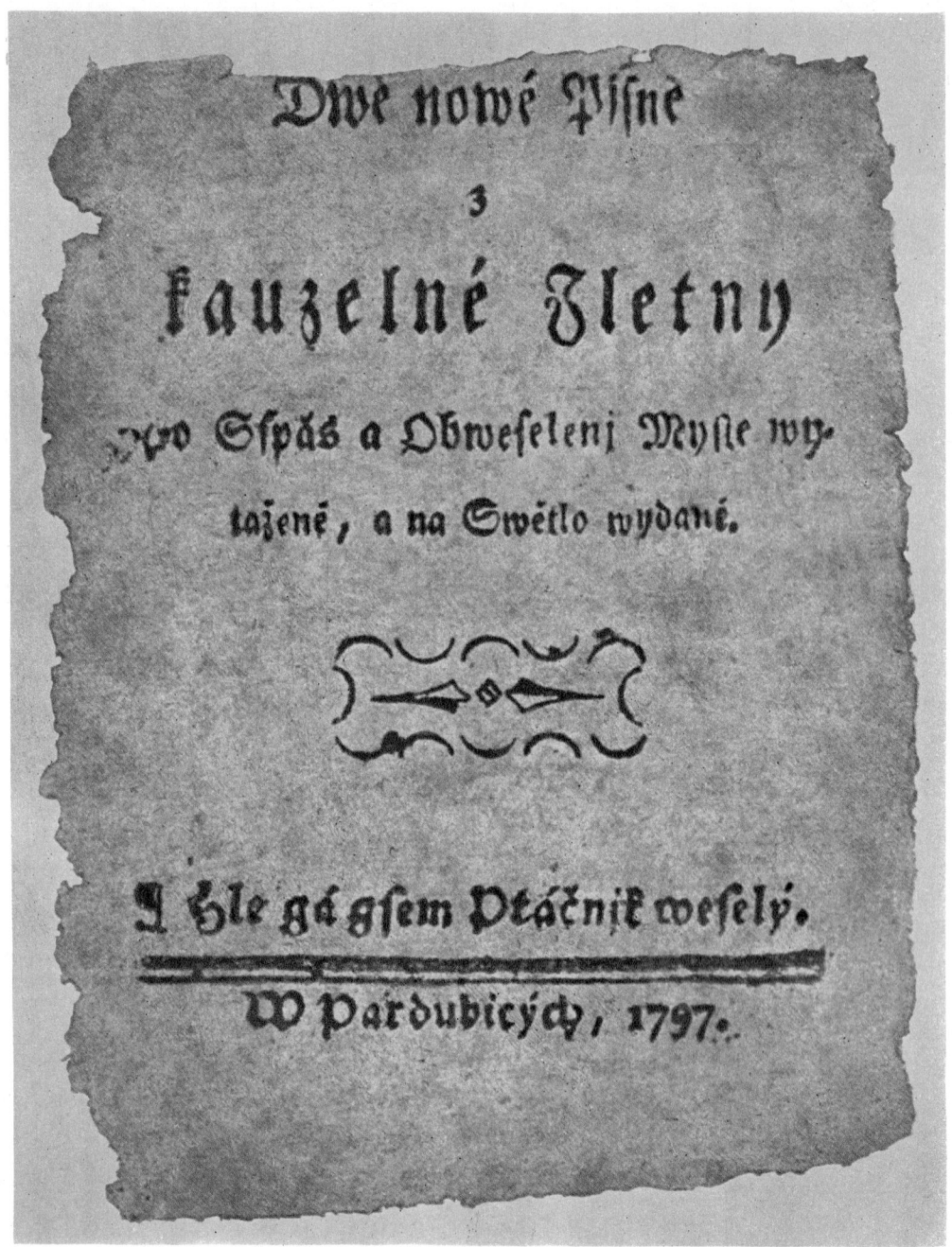

**THE MAGIC FLUTE**

*Title page of the text of two of the most popular arias (Papageno's and Monostatos's) published as Showman's songs in Pardubice in 1797. This proves how popular Mozart's music was among different levels of society.*

*PAMINA Du hier!— Gütige Götter*
*Achzehenter Auftritt II Act*

## PERIOD STAGING OF THE MAGIC FLUTE

*During his last visit to Prague Mozart's head was buzzing with the themes from The Magic Flute*
*and he played his friends at Bertramka the quintet of Tamino, Papageno and the three ladies.*

A rare colour etching by Petr and Josef Schaffer. Prague, Music Department of the National Museum.

### W. A. MOZART
*Silhouette from the set marking the première of Don Giovanni.*
Bertramka, Mozart and Dušek Memorial.

J. N. HUMMEL.

## JAN NEPOMUK HUMMEL
*Excellent pianist and composer, a pupil of Mozart (1778–1837). During his stay in Prague in 1783 he and his father were guests of the Dušeks.*
Etching of the period. Prague, Music Department of the National Museum.

## BILL ANNOUNCING HUMMEL'S PERFORMANCE IN PRAGUE
*He played at the Konvikt Hall, March 15th, 1795.*
Prague, Music Department of the National Museum.

# Nachricht

für

## Liebhaber und Freunde

der

## Tonkunst.

———————

Herr JOHANN HUMMEL, 15 Jahr alt, ein Virtuos auf dem Forte piano und Schüler des so berühmten und seel. Kapellmeister Mozart, ist von seinen fünfjährigen Reisen hier angekommen. Er ist entschlossen seine musikalischen Talente, die er zwar schon vor 6 Jahren im Hochgräflich Thunischen Theater allhier bewiesen, aber jetzt mit so glücklichen Erfolg ausgebildet hat, daß er auf seinen Reisen durch ganz England, Schottland Holland, Dänemark, im ganzen deutschen Reiche, und am meisten Höfen Europens, wie auch verschiedenemale im k. k. National-Hoftheater zu Wien, allgemein bewundert wurde, auch hier den Freunden und Liebhabern der Musik in einer musikalischen

ACADEMIE,

welche künftigen Sonntag den 15ten März 1795. im Konviktsaale gehalten werden wird, die Ehre haben zu zeigen. Der entscheidende Geschmak, den die hiesigen edlen Bewohner Prags in Werken der Kunst besitzen, wird ihn auffodern, sich zu bemühen, auch hier den Beyfall zu erringen, den er sonst zu erhalten so glücklich war.

Das Mehrere wird der Anschlagzettel anzeigen.

# Leben

des

## K. K. Kapellmeisters

## Wolfgang Gottlieb Mozart,

nach

Originalquellen beschrieben

von

### Franz Niemtschek,

Professor am Prager Kleinseit. Gymnasium.

Prag 1798.
In der Herrlischen Buchhandlung.

FIRST BIOGRAPHY OF MOZART
*by František Xaver Němeček, published in Prague in 1798.*
Prague, University Library.

W. A. MOZART

*Detail of the engraving on the title page of the piano arrangement of Mozart's E flat
Symphony, published by Jan Vencl in Prague.*
Engraving by J. Berka. Prague, Music Department of the National Museum.

Stahlstich von Carl Mayer Nbg.

ABBÉ GELINEK

JOSEF JELÍNEK

*Composer and piano virtuoso (1758 – 1825). He published numerous variations and*
*fantasies on themes from Mozart's composition.*
Steel engraving by C. Mayer. Prague, Music Department of the National Museum.

# VARIATIONS
## Pour le Piano-Forte
### sur un Duo de l'Opera la Clemenza di Tito
### Composées et Dediées
## à Mademoiselle Angelique de Deyma
#### par
## L'ABBÉ GELINEK.

No.62 ———————— * ———————— Pr.18gl.

### Leipsic et Berlin.
#### au Bureau des arts et d'industrie.
178.

VARIATIONS FOR PIANO
*on the theme of Mozart's La Clemenza di Tito by J. Jelinek.*
Prague, Music Department of the National Museum.

## FANTASIA PATHETICA

(op. 9). Tomášek wrote of this composition of his: "Because of my special delight in Mozart's works I adapted the main theme of this work from the superbly beautiful piano fantasy in C minor..."
Prague, Music Department of the National Museum.

## VÁCLAV JAN TOMÁŠEK

An outstanding composer of the pre-Smetana period (1774–1850).
Oil-painting by A. Machek. Prague, National Gallery.

CHILDREN'S SONGS BY V. MAŠEK AND F. X. DUŠEK
*dedicated to Louisa and Jeanetta the Countesses Clam-Gallas,*

*with mezottin etchings of both countesses by J. Berka.*
Prague, Music Department of the National Museum.

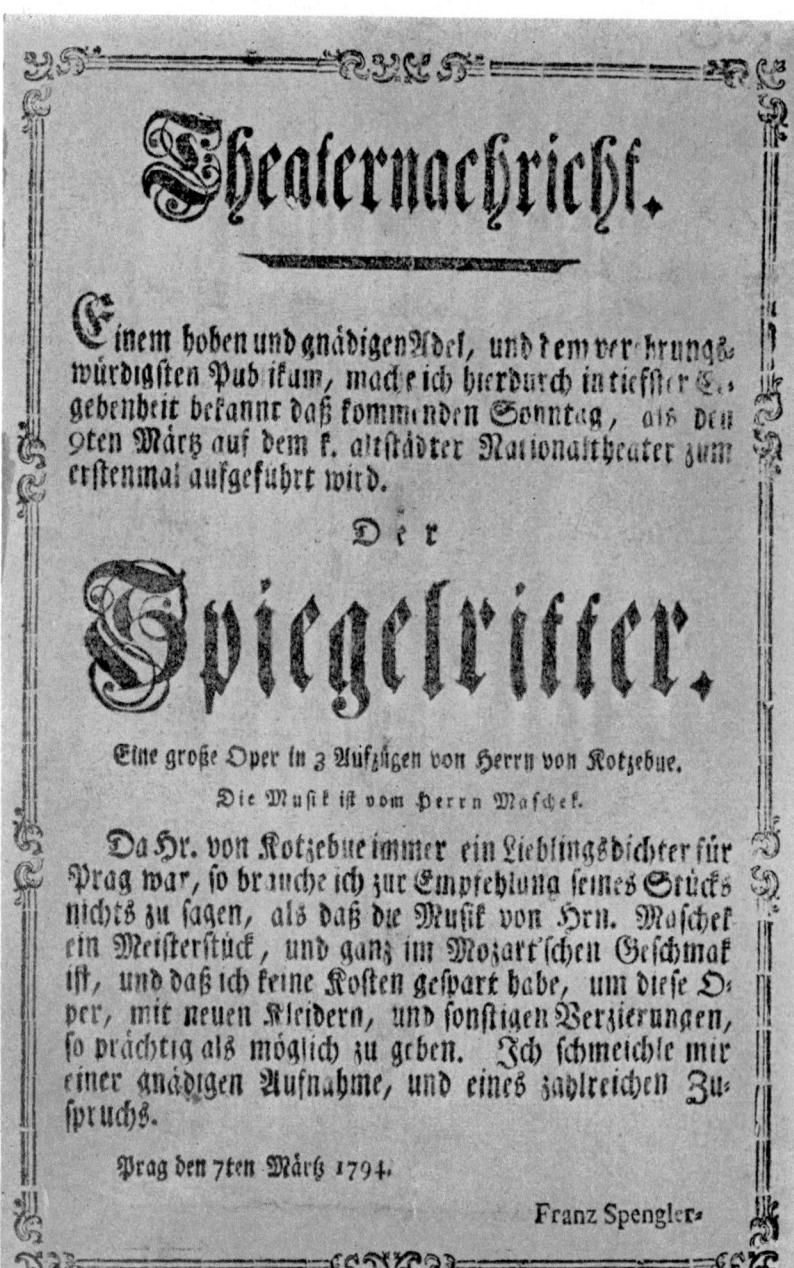

**BILL ANNOUNCING THE PREMIÈRE**
*of Mašek's opera Der Spiegelritter, 9th March, 1794, which reads
"...the music by Mr. Mašek is masterly and is entirely in the spirit of
Mozart..."*
Prague, Music Department of the National Museum.

FRANTIŠEK XAVER DUŠEK
*(1731–1799). Silhouette.*
Bertramka, Mozart and Dušek Memorial.

PIANO ARRANGEMENT OF MOZART'S E FLAT SYMPHONY (K. V. 543)
*by the organist of St. Vitus's Jan Vencl (1759–1831) dated 1794, dedicated to Dušek and his ad-mirers, with a portrait of Mozart.*
Engraving by J. Berka. Prague, Music Department of the National Museum.

Gezeichnet von L. Janscha.    Gestochen von C. Postl.

*Ansicht des Wissehrad und Podskal von Laurenziberg in Prag. Vue de Wissehrad et Podskal, du coté de la Montagne St. Laurent a Prague.*

PRAGUE
*View from the Kinský's Gardens over the Vltava valley and the Smíchov district.*
Engraving by K. Postel, after Jauch. Bertramka, Mozart and Dušek Memorial.

Ferrando, im 2.<sup>ten</sup> Costume aus der Oper: Mädchentreue,
(Cosi fan tutte) gespielt von Hrn. Grünbaum. Act 2. Sc. 9.
Verrathen! — verschmacht! — vergessen bin ich!

**FERRANDO'S COSTUME**
*from the opera Cosi fan Tutte, from contemporary
engravings.*
Bertramka, Mozart and Dušek Memorial.

Mit hoher und gnädigster Bewilligung

Wird heute Dienstag den 26. April 1791.

# MADAME DUSCHEK
die Ehre haben,

im königl. Nationaltheater

# Eine Musikalische
# ACADEMIE
zu geben.

Vorkommende Stücke:

1tens. Eine Symphonie von Herrn Girovetz.

2tens. Eine Allegro Arie von Herrn Cimarosa.

3tens. Ein Stück aus einer Simphonie.

4tens. Eine ganz neu verfertigte große Scene von Herrn Mozart.

5tens. Ein Konzert auf dem Forte piano von Hrn. Mozart gespielt von Hrn. Witassek.

6tens. Ein Rondo von Herrn Mozart mit obligaten Bassete-Horn.

7tens. Den Beschluß macht ein Stück aus einer Simphonie.

Preiße der Plätze:

| | | | |
|---|---|---|---|
| Eine Loge im ersten Rang | 1 halben Souverain. | Auf den zweyten Parterre | 24 Kr. |
| Eine Loge im zweyten Rang | 1 Ducaten. | Gallerielogen die Person | 20 kr. |
| Parterre noble | 1 Fl. | Auf dem letzten Platz | 10 kr. |
| Das löbliche Militair zahlt wie gewöhnlich. | | | |

Der Anfang ist um 6 Uhr.          Das Ende um 8 Uhr.

BILL ANNOUNCING THE CONCERT AT THE NOSTITZ
THEATRE
*26th April, 1791, at which Josefa Dušek sang Mozart's works.*
Prague, Music Department of the National Museum.

*Josepha Duschek.*

### JOSEFA DUŠEK, NÉE HAMBACHER

*(1754–1824), famous singer, first pupil, later wife of F. X. Dušek. She not only enchanted the select society of court salons by her art, but also Mozart and Beethoven.*

Engraving by A. Clar, 1796, after Haake. Prague, Music Department of the National Museum.

THE DUŠEKS’ APARTMENT IN PRAGUE
*in Upper Malá Strana Square.*
Detail of colour etching by Filip and František Heger, 1794. Prague Museum.

### VOJTĚCH JÍROVEC

*Popular conductor and operatic composer (1763–1850). His symphonies, which were on the programme of Josefa Dušek's concert, were first introduced by Mozart at his concert.*

Contemporary etching. Prague, Music Department of the National Museum.

**ENAMELLED SWEET BOX**
*complete with opera glasses, a wedding present to Josefa Dušek from her husband.*
Bertramka, Mozart and Dušek Memorial. Property of the Industrial Arts Museum in Prague.

**JOHANN GOTTLIEB NAUMANN**
*Composer and court conductor in Dresden (1741–1801). He was several times the guest of the Dušeks in Prague, where he also met Mozart in 1787 and 1791. He wrote La dama soldato for Mrs Dušek in 1786.*
Oil-painting by O. Graf, Bertramka, Mozart and Dušek Memorial.

MANUSCRIPT OF THE MESSIAH
*by G. F. Handel into which Mozart wrote the parts for wind instruments.*
Prague, Music Department of the National Museum.

**Der Messias.**

Ein
Oratorium aus dem englischen
Texte übersetzt.

Aufgeführt zu Prag am 1. April 1804.

Zum Besten der Wittwen = und Waisenversorgungs=
anstalt der Tonkünstlergesellschaft.

Prag, gedruckt bey Johann Diesbach.

Die Musik ist ursprünglich von dem berühm=
ten Fr. G. Händel gesetzt; von W. A. Mozart
durch angemessene Umänderung und Bearbeitung der
Instrumentalpartie dem Kunstgeschmacke unserer Zeit
näher gebracht.

Mad. Dussek — Canto
Mad.l Batka — Alt.
Mr. Kussy, Tenorist
Mr. Woytissek. Bassist
l Theola, geb. Gladroesy

**LIBRETTO OF THE MESSIAH**

*with the signatures of the performers who also included Josefa Dušek. It is stated in the libretto that*
*"the music is originally by the famous G. F. Handel: by suitable alterations and modifications of the*
*instrumental parts W. A. Mozart has made it more acceptable to the artistic taste of our time."*
Prague, Museum of National Literature.

### THE SONS OF W. A. MOZART
*Karl Thomas (1784–1858) and Franz Xaver (1791–1844). F. X. Němeček and the Dušeks together took care of them after Mozart's death.*
Oil-painting by H. Hansen. Salzburg, Internationale Stiftung Mozarteum.

W. A. MOZART
Unknown master from the first half of the 19th century.
Prague, Music Department of the National Museum.

FRANZ XAVER MOZART
*called by his mother after his father, Wolfgang Amadeus, was a musician and a popular
teacher. He also appeared as a pianist in Prague.*
Lithograph after Kriehuber, 1844. Prague, Music Department of the National Museum.

**KARLOVY VARY**
*where Mozart's younger son, Franz Xaver Wolfgang Amadeus, died.*
Contemporary coloured lithograph by E. Gurk. Prague, Dvořák Museum.

TOMB OF MOZART'S SON AT KARLOVY VARY
Contemporary lithograph. Bertramka, Mozart and Dušek Memorial.

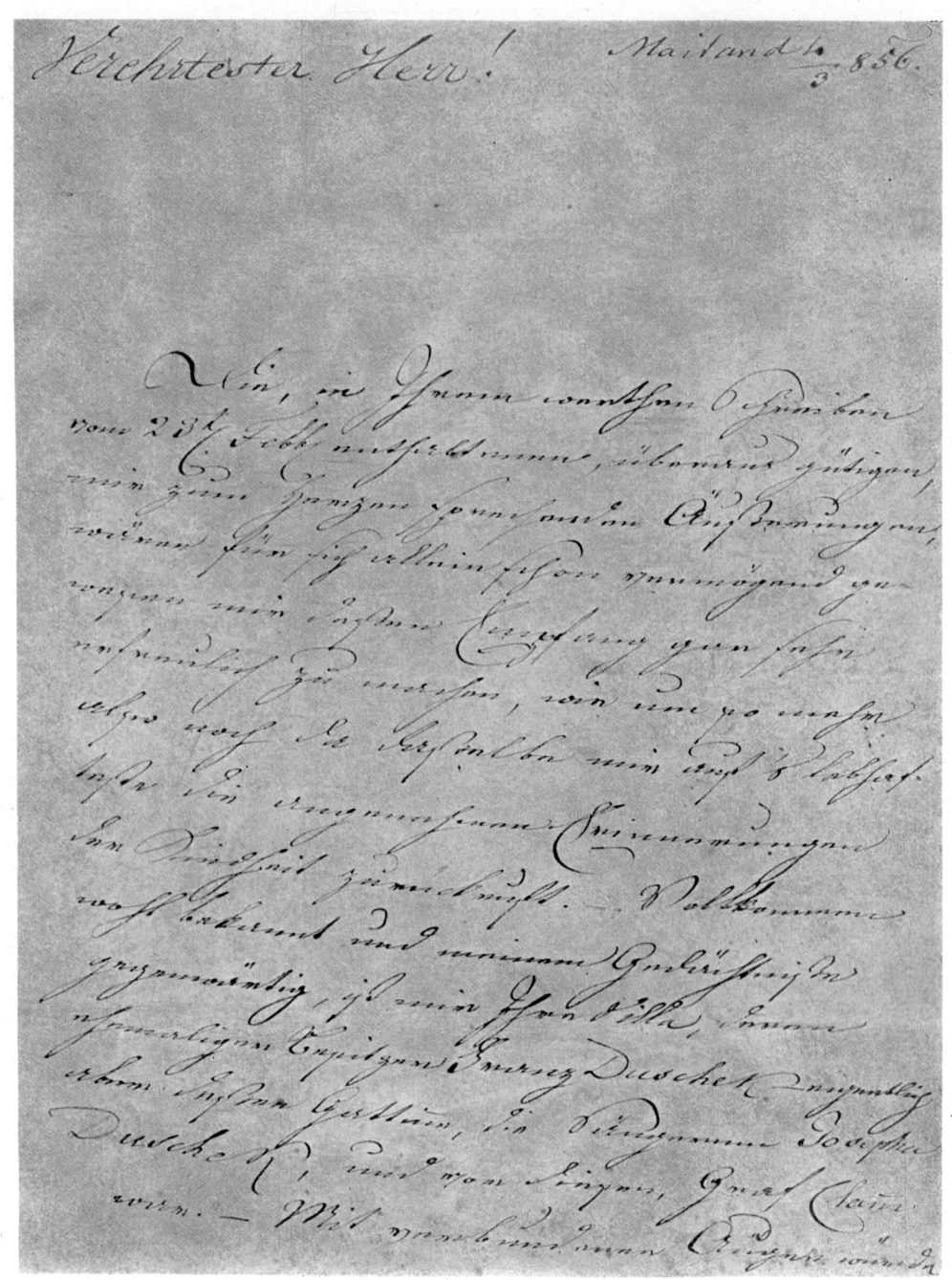

FIRST PAGE OF A LETTER BY KARL MOZART
*to Adolf Popelka in which he speaks of his childhood in Prague and the Bertramka.*
Bertramka, Mozart and Dušek Memorial.

W. A. MOZART

*Painting by an unknown artist between 1810–20 for Count Boss-Waldek. Presumably*
*Mozart's sons were his model.*
Bertramka, Mozart and Dušek Memorial.

**THE BEGINNING OF BEDŘICH SMETANA'S CADENZA**
*to Mozart's piano concerto in D minor (K. V. 466). Mozart was a shining example
to Smetana throughout his life.*
Prague, Bedřich Smetana Museum.

BEDŘICH SMETANA
*Founder of Czech national opera (1824—1884).*
Contemporary lithograph after G. Solomon. Prague, Bedřich Smetana Museum.

ANTONÍN DVOŘÁK

*Famous Czech composer (1841–1904). In his serenades for strings (op. 22), for wind instruments (op. 44) and in The Jacobin (scene with the village teacher, Benda), Dvořák also proclaims his fidelity to the Mozart tradition.*

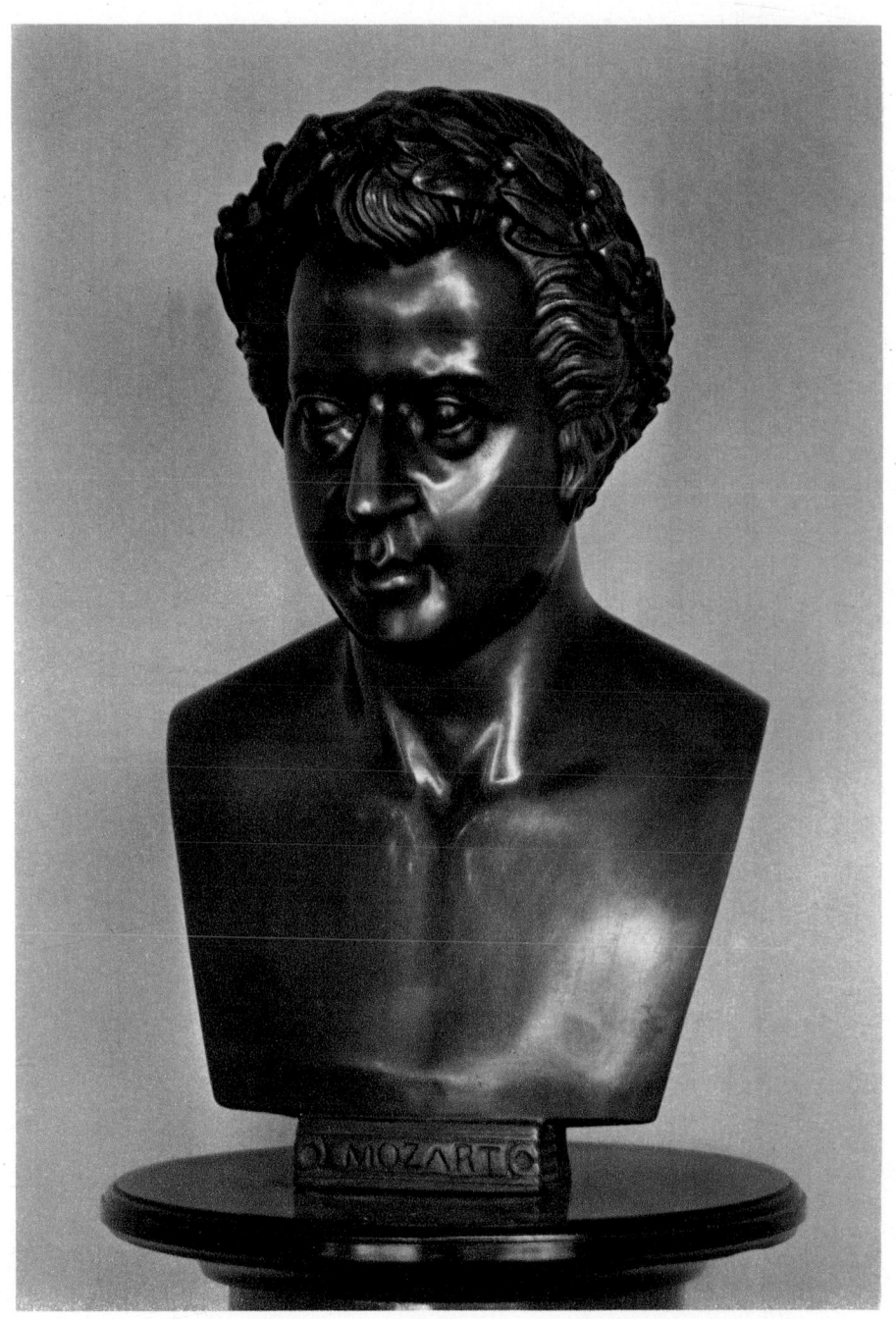

BRONZE BUST OF MOZART
*by Emanuel Marx, 1837.*
Bertramka, Mozart and Dušek Memorial.

BUST OF MOZART IN WHITE BISCUIT
The work of the Prague modeller, A. Popp, in the forties of the last century.
Bertramka, Mozart and Dušek Memorial.

SKETCHES FOR COSTUMES FOR MOZART'S BASTIEN AND BASTIENNE
*performed in Terezín concentration camp. The producer, F. Zelenka, died on the "death march".*
Prague, Dramatic Art Department of the National Museum.

PAPAGENA FROM THE MAGIC FLUTE
*Metal mould from the Nový Jáchymov foundries in the 19th century.*
Bertramka, Mozart and Dušek Memorial.

W·A·MOZART

1756                    1956

**PRODUCTION OF THE MARRIAGE OF FIGARO**
*Design by J. Svoboda; the Mozart Week which opened the anniversary ce-
lebrations was inaugurated by this production at the Tyl (formerly Nostitz)
Theatre in Prague.*

**POSTER**
*issued throughout Czechoslovakia for the celebrations of the 200th anniver-
sary of the birth of Mozart.*
Design A. Novotná-Guttfreundová.

"THEY EVEN WHISTLE FIGARO..."

*Cyril Bouda's illustration to Karel Koval's book Mozart in Prague which was
published to mark the Mozart Jubilee in 1956.*

THE BERTRAMKA

*in the Smíchov district of Prague, where Mozart spent some of the happiest days of his life. The Mozart and Dušek Memorial was set up here in the Jubilee Year 1956.*

Water-colour by A. Kirnig, 1887. Bertramka, Mozart and Dušek Memorial.

THE BERTRAMKA

*View from the courtyard.*

W. A. MOZART

*Sandstone bust in the garden of the Bertramka, by Tomáš Seidan, 1876.*

THE BERTRAMKA

*Mozart's rooms.*

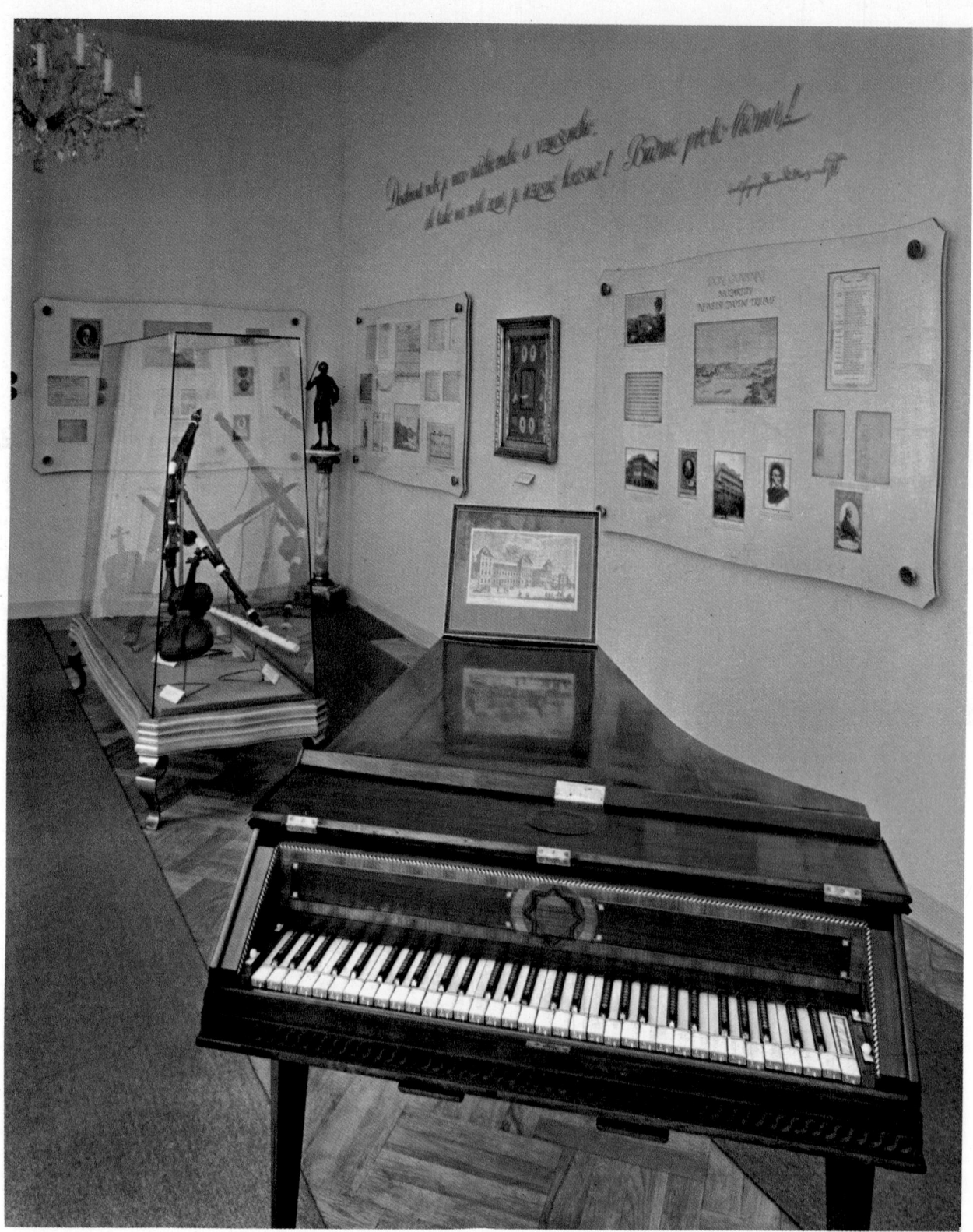

**THE BERTRAMKA**
*The Dušeks' hall.*

**THE BERTRAMKA**
*Exhibition of musical instruments and relics of Mozart.*

*Illustration by K. Müller from the Mozart novel by the Prague writer Louis Fürnberg, entitled Amadé and Casanova. The setting of the novel is the Bertramka.*

THE GARDEN AT THE BERTRAMKA
*with the stone table at which Mozart is said to have frequently sat.*

**BRONZE COMMEMORATION MEDALLION**

*with a bust of Mozart and the Nostitz Theatre (now the Tyl Theatre) by J. T. Fischer, on the occasion of the 200th anniversary of Mozart's birth.*

## POSTAGE STAMPS

*for the Mozart celebrations at the Prague Spring 1956 International Music Festival.*
Engraving by S. Jindra from a design by K. Svolinský.

JUNE 2ND, 1956

*Mozart's Coronation Mass and Requiem being performed at St. Vitus's Cathedral during the Prague Spring International Music Festival before an audience of around 6.000.*

### THE TYL THEATRE

*(formerly the Nostitz Theatre) where the Prague celebrations of the 200th anniversary of Mozart's were held, beginning with the performance of Don Giovanni and inauguration of the International Conference on the works of Mozart.*

RUDOLF ASMUS
*in the role of Leporello in Don Giovanni in the performance at the Tyl Theatre on 27th January,*
*1956.*
Engraving by K. Dostál.

**IN HONOUR OF W. A. MOZART**
Sketch by C. Bouda. Gobelin for the Bertramka.

**W. A. MOZART**
*Design for gobelins by Jan Bauch, completed on the occasion of the 200th anniversary of Mozart's birth.*
The gobelins were worked by the Art-Crafts workshops in Jindřichův Hradec, director Marie
Teinitzerová.

W. A. MOZART

Charcoal drawing by František Hofman.

PRAGA REGINA MUSICAE
Gobelin design by C. Bouda.

S. M. IMPERATRIX IN BOHEMIÆ REGINAM SOLEMNITER CORONATA DIE 12 SEPTEMBRIS 1791

**CORONATION OF THE WIFE OF EMPEROR LEOPOLD II**

*on 12th September, 1791, in Prague.*

Coloured etching, Prague, privately owned.

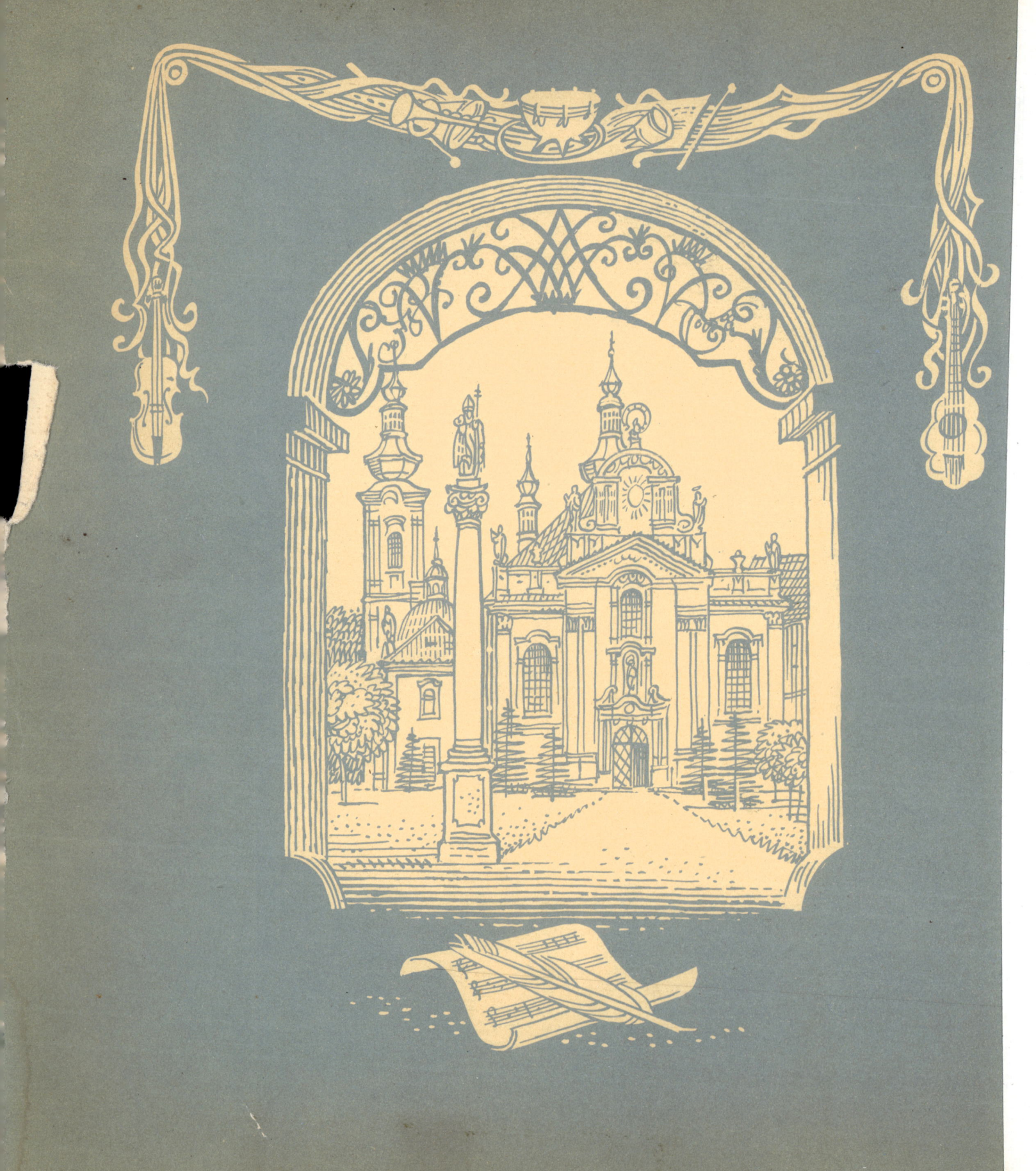